"I am not playing kissy-face with you in public, Harper."

"Think about it," said Luke. "You want to deflect attention from your business. I don't want reporters digging too deep into my presence in the U.K. So we bend the truth to work for both of us."

"No."

"The media wants a show. We give 'em one."

"No."

Exasperated, Luke folded his arms. "Okay, let's hear some alternatives."

"I can think of several," said Dayna. "The first involves you ejecting from your cockpit without a parachute."

"What's number two?"

"You ejecting without your helmet."

His lips twitched. "Is there a number three?"

No, damnit, there wasn't. Not one that didn't require death or dismemberment, anyway. Dayna fumed for several moments before admitting as much.

"So where does that leave us?" Luke asked.

"Playing kissy-face in public," she conceded.

Dear Reader,

Some years ago, my husband and I took a trip to Scotland and decided to play a round of golf on St. Andrews's venerable Old Course, the birthplace of golf. Relatively new to the game, we didn't realize folks reserved tee times as much as a year in advance. Luckily, there had just been a cancellation and the starter was able to get us right on the course.

Wish I could say I finished the round, but I lost my last ball to the man-eating gorse on hole seventeen! What a fabulous experience, though. And what great fodder for a book, although I didn't know then I was going to become a writer.

Hope you share the thrill of glorious St. Andrews along with my intrepid hero and heroine as they battle bullets and bad guys in this latest CODE NAME: DANGER thriller.

All my best,

Merline Lovelace

MERLINE LOVELACE

Match Play

Romantic

SUSPENSE

SILHOUETTE BOOKS

ISBN-13: 978-0-373-27570-0
ISBN-10:   0-373-27570-6

MATCH PLAY

Visit Silhouette Books at www.eHarlequin.com

Printed in U.S.A.

MERLINE LOVELACE

A retired air force colonel, Merline Lovelace served at bases all over the world, including tours in Taiwan, Vietnam and at the Pentagon. When she hung up her uniform for the last time, she decided to combine her love of adventure with her flair for storytelling, basing many of her tales on her experiences in the service.

Since then she's produced more than seventy action-packed sizzlers, many of which have made the *USA TODAY* and Waldenbooks bestseller lists. The CODE NAME: DANGER books are among her favorites. Check Merline's Web site, www.merlinelovelace.com, for news, contests and publication dates.

To my sweetie, with whom I've shared so many wonderful adventures and jaunts around the world. Here's to all the fun trips yet to come!

Chapter 1

"That's all we have?"

Undercover operative Dayna Duncan lifted a sun-bleached brow. Her green eyes, so vivid against her tanned skin, locked on her boss.

"Wu Kim Li is playing in the Women's International Pro-Am Charity Tournament and whispered an urgent message to another golfer that her father is flying to Scotland to watch her compete?"

"That's all we have," Nick Jensen confirmed.

Nick, code name Lightning, had run the ultra-secret organization known only as OMEGA for more years than he wanted to count now. It was headquartered in a brick town house just off Massachusetts Avenue, in the heart of Washington, D.C.'s embassy district. A discreet bronze plaque beside the front door identified the building as home to the offices of the President's Special Envoy—one of those meaningless titles given to well-heeled contributors to campaign war chests. Not more than a handful of insiders knew the Special Envoy also served as director of an organization so small and so secret that its agents were activated only at the request of the President himself.

One of those agents was preparing to go into the field now. Dayna Duncan, code name Rogue, had arrived at the town house via a secret underground access and been whisked up to OMEGA's high-tech Control Center mere moments ago. This wasn't Dayna's first op, by any means, but from the little she'd heard so far, it sounded as though it might be right up her alley.

Lightning's next question confirmed her guess. "What kind of handicap are you carrying these days?"

"A two," she replied, scrunching her nose in disgust. Golf was more of a hobby now than the passion it had once been, but Dayna still played to win.

"You do know," her boss drawled, "most of us weekend duffers would kill for a two handicap?"

"I'll be back to scratch by the Pro-Am Charity

Tournament," she predicted confidently. "You *are* sending me to Scotland to get close to Wu and her daddy, aren't you?"

"I am."

"Yes!"

A former college all-star athlete, Dayna had twice won Olympic gold in the controlled mayhem known as white-water kayaking. She took her code name from the Rogue River in Oregon, where she'd first learned to run rapids. Her current job as a consultant at one of the nation's foremost outdoor sports-training centers gave her both flexibility and the perfect cover for her OMEGA assignments.

Especially this one. Eighteen-year-old golf prodigy Wu Kim Li was one of those international celebrities everyone loved to hate. Incredibly skilled, obnoxiously temperamental, the North Korean won as many fans by sinking a long putt as she turned off by her tirades when she missed a short one. But it was the golfer's father who had captured OMEGA's attention.

"What's the story on Dr. Wu?" she asked. "I know he's some kind of a scientist working on hush-hush stuff."

Nick flicked a switch and filled the Control Center's wall-size screen with the intent, unsmiling face of Wu Kim Li's father.

"This is our most recent photo of Dr. Wu Xia-Dong. The photo was hard to come by, as he hasn't traveled outside North Korea in almost a decade. His government keeps him on a short leash. No surprise, considering he's one of their foremost nuclear weapons engineers."

"Uh-oh. I'm guessing that doesn't make him real popular with the White House."

"To put it mildly."

Relations between the United States and North Korea, always shaky, had deteriorated steadily in recent months over Korea's stubborn determination to develop nuclear weapons. The situation had become so tense that the State Department had warned U.S. citizens to think twice about doing business with or traveling to North Korea. As Dayna studied the face on the screen, she wondered how much Dr. Wu had contributed to those tensions.

"What's the thinking?" she asked. "Why did Kim Li whisper that urgent message about her father's attendance at the golf tournament in Scotland?"

"The CIA has picked up subtle vibes that Wu is chafing under the constraints his government imposes on him. They're convinced he wants to defect. Your task will be to find out if that's true and, if so, effect the escape."

Nick didn't have to tell his agent how absolutely vital this op was to U.S. national security. Her low whistle indicated she'd grasped the implications immediately.

"What about the daughter? Is she in on this, too?"

"We think so."

He brought another photo up on the screen. This one captured Wu Kim Li in midswing, displaying the perfect form and incredible power that had led the media to christen her Tigress Wu.

"As you well know," Nick said, "she makes millions in product endorsements. Since she lives in a Communist state, however, only a fraction of those revenues come to her personally."

"If that," Dayna commented. "I've competed against athletes from Communist countries. The State produces them, the State reaps the reward. Particularly North Korea. They won't let their athletes train anywhere but in their own country."

"Precisely. And Wu has more than product endorsements to tempt her. She's hinted that she's interested in a possible career in the movies."

"She certainly has the face and figure for it," Dayna agreed. "Too bad she's such a little bitch. Hollywood will have trouble casting her as anything but a werewolf."

Nick left the photo on the screen as he studied his

field agent. Wu Kim Li wasn't the only athlete with the face and figure to make it big in Hollywood. Rogue's shoulder-length tumble of honey-colored hair framed a face dominated by sculpted cheekbones and wide, forest-green eyes. Regular and strenuous exercise had honed her body to a perfect symmetry of line and curve. Posters of her lithe form molded by the wet suit she'd worn in her last run for Olympic gold still sold for megabucks on eBay.

"Think you can get past Wu's bitchiness and gain her trust?"

"The first task, sure. The second task might be tougher. I'll find some way to connect, though."

Lightning nodded. Rogue was one of his top operatives. If anyone could crack through Wu Kim Li's ring of bodyguards and watchdogs, she could.

"While you work the daughter, Hawkeye will work the father."

Surprised, Rogue flicked a glance at the world map on the wall of the Control Center. Signals sent via GPS satellites pinpointed the exact location of the three OMEGA agents currently in the field. One of them was Mike Callahan, code name Hawkeye.

"Isn't Hawk in Algeria?"

"He is, but he's about to wrap things up there. He'll fly from Algiers and connect with you in Scotland."

"Good. We work well together."

No surprise there, Nick thought. A former military cop and world-class sharpshooter, Mike Callahan had racked up almost as many trophies and titles in his field of expertise as Dayna had in hers. They had nothing but respect for each other—on and off the job.

Now, for the tricky part.

Hitting the switch, Nick took Wu Kim Li's face off the screen and replaced it with an aerial map of Scotland. The town of St. Andrews sat midway up the east coast, at the tip of a peninsula that jutted into the North Sea. Zooming in, Nick focused on the Royal Air Force Base a few kilometers from the town.

"If you confirm the Wus want to defect, the best place for the extraction is here, at RAF Leuchars."

Dayna agreed with his assessment. "It's been years since I played St. Andrews, but I remember seeing British fighters landing and taking off from the base."

"British fighters aren't the only planes bedded down at RAF Leuchars. The U.S. also has a detachment of B-2 Stealth bombers there."

"I didn't know that."

"Few people do. The British government is under intense fire for its support of the Iraqi War. A growing antiwar movement doesn't want to see that support continue or expand. When word leaked that the B-2s might go in at RAF Fairford, in the south of England, suspected al-Qaeda sympathizers infiltrated what

began as a peaceful protest march and turned it into
a near riot. As a result, the U.S. and U.K. govern-
ments decided to bed the B-2s down farther north,
outside St. Andrews. So far the presence of the
bombers at RAF Leuchars has remained an uncon-
firmed rumor among the local populace."

He swiveled his chair, turning away from the
screen to watch Rogue's reaction to his next comment.

"We have a detachment of USAF aircrews and
support personnel at RAF Leuchars. One of the pilots
is Captain Luke Harper."

Rogue was good. Damned good. Her green eyes
showed only a bare flicker of emotion.

"Luke and I are ancient history."

Not that ancient. The romance between one
of America's most promising—and photogenic—
athletes and her handsome young lieutenant had
made for great TV spots during the hype leading
up to the 2004 Olympics. They were the perfect
couple—the tanned, charismatic golden girl with the
flashing smile and infectious enthusiasm for her sport
and the air-force pilot she'd met while they were
both students at the University of Colorado.

Their romance died an abrupt death six months
before the Olympics. In subsequent interviews,
Dayna had turned aside the inevitable questions
about her love life with a laugh and vague references

to the difficulty of sustaining a long-distance relationship. There had been no lack of men in her life in the years since, but none had lasted long or generated the kind of intense media interest as her first and very public love.

"I can have Harper transferred off the base if you think he might compromise this op in any way," Lightning told her. "Just say the word."

Rogue had been in the business too long to dismiss the suggestion without giving it serious consideration. Lips pursed, she examined the issue from all angles.

"The only problem I see is if the media picks up on his presence and connects him to the Stealth Bombers."

"Security at the base is airtight. As far as the general public knows, the USAF personnel stationed there are attached to the RAF fighter wing as part of an exchange program. I'm more concerned that Harper's presence might impact your performance in the tournament."

Rogue didn't hesitate this time. "Breaking up with Luke Harper didn't throw me off stride in the Olympics. After all these years, the mere fact that he's stationed at an air base a few kilometers away isn't going to affect my game."

Which brought them around to another touchy subject, one Lightning suspected might generate even more sparks.

The Women's International Pro-Am Charity Tournament was open to any amateur or professional golfer willing to put up the ten-thousand-dollar entry fee. While the main object was to raise money for the International Red Cross, it was still a competition. All entrants could play the first two qualifying rounds. Only those posting the lowest scores would make the cut for the final two rounds.

"Barring some unforeseen disaster," he said, bracing himself for the explosion he knew would come, "Wu Kim Li will compete in the final rounds. We need to make sure you do, too."

"*Make* sure?" Deep creases slashed into her forehead. "You're not suggesting we rig the tournament, are you?"

"Not exactly."

"C'mon, boss! I've never cheated in my life and don't intend to start now. I know my golf game is a little rusty, but I'll make the cut."

"I'm sure you will, too. Assuming worst-case scenario, however…"

"There is no worst-case scenario," Rogue countered stubbornly. "I *will* make the cut."

"Assuming worst-case scenario," Nick continued with unruffled calm, "we need to make sure you at least tie with the last-place finisher in the qualifying rounds so you *both* go on to the championship round."

She didn't like it. He could see disgust written all over her face. She'd come around, though. She understood the stakes in this game and would balance her sporting instincts against the needs of the United States.

It took a few minutes. Her teeth stayed locked. A muscle twitched in the side of her jaw. Her fingers drummed a furious tattoo on the console.

"Okay," she finally conceded. "Assuming worst-case scenario, how do we pull it off?"

A rueful smile spread across Nick's face. His wife, the guru of all things electronic for OMEGA and several other government agencies, had jumped at this challenge. Mackenzie was huddled with the wizards in OMEGA'S Field Dress Unit now.

"Mac is waiting for you upstairs. She's been working on several devices."

"Uh-oh."

Uh-oh was right. Thankfully, FDU's labs were sound-, shock wave- and bombproof. Its walls would contain the blast when Rogue saw what Mac and her diabolical geniuses had come up with.

Hours later, a fuming Dayna paced the first-floor reception area.

"You won't believe what Mackenzie wants to stick in my golf bag! GPS-guided balls. Distance-finding sunglasses. A super-charged three iron, for God's sake."

Lightning's temporary executive assistant sat behind her elegant Louis XV desk. Gillian Ridgeway, daughter of two of OMEGA's former superstars, played a mean game of golf herself. Amusement and sympathy lit her blue eyes.

"You won't need any of those aids."

"Damn straight, I won't."

Jilly continued to make sympathetic noises until Dayna worked through her snit.

"Sorry," the agent said with a wry smile. "I just needed to let off a little steam."

"That's what I'm here for."

Actually, Gillian Ridgeway was there to fill in for Elizabeth Wells, longtime executive assistant to several of OMEGA's directors. Elizabeth had undergone hip-replacement surgery the week after Jilly returned from a State Department assignment in Beijing. On leave from State and unsure whether she wanted to become a career bureaucrat, Jilly had offered to fill in for Elizabeth.

Black-haired, blue-eyed and as stunning as she was vivacious, she soon wrapped OMEGA's male agents around her little finger. The female agents liked her, too, which said even more for her sparkling personality.

She and Dayna had grown especially close. The two women were almost the same age and both enjoyed sports. They teamed up for golf or tennis whenever Rogue was in D.C. and routinely skunked their opponents. They'd also shared a few locker-room secrets. So Dayna wasn't surprised when Gillian made a too-casual observation.

"I understand Hawkeye is working this op with you."

"That's right. He's flying in from Algiers. We meet up in Scotland."

"Say hi for me, will you?"

"I will, but only if you promise to stop torturing the poor man."

"Torturing him?" Gillian assumed an expression of wide-eyed innocence. *"Moi?"*

"Come off it, Jilly. You know you lay on a double dose of sultry whenever Hawk's around. Despite that, he still thinks of you as the gawky teenager he taught to shoot."

"Maybe," she replied with a small smirk, "and maybe not. Just tell him hello for me."

When Dayna hooked up with Hawk in her suite at one of St. Andrews' venerable old hotels, she dutifully relayed the message.

"Gillian said to say hi. And you look like hell."

Hawk shot her a surprised look from sunken, red-rimmed eyes. "Jilly said that?"

"The last bit came from me. What happened in Algiers?"

"Sand, sand and more sand." A smile slipped through the bristly beard sprouting on his cheeks and chin. "But we got Mustafa."

Whooping, Dayna leaned across the coffee table to punch her fellow agent in the shoulder.

"Score one for our side!"

His smile took over the rest of his face. No one would classify Hawk as handsome. His features were too rugged and his tough, don't-mess-with-me demeanor too intimidating. But when he relaxed and let the real Mike Callahan show through, Dayna could understand why Gillian was so determined to make the man see her as something other than a gangly teen.

"It took a little longer than expected," he admitted ruefully. "I had to leave the bastard hanging across the saddle of a camel to get here in time for this tournament. Speaking of which…"

Scraping a palm across his bristly chin, he made the abrupt mental shift so necessary for survival in their business.

"Any more definitive word on whether the Wus really intend to defect?"

"None. All we have to go on is that cryptic message from Kim Li." Dayna shuffled through the folder of material she'd prepared for him. "Here's your registration packet and a detailed agenda."

The International Pro-Am Charity Tournament had grown into one of the biggest events in women's golf. Spread over an entire week, the schedule was crammed with money-raising activities. The public could watch the practice round, first two preliminary rounds and final championship rounds—all for a fee, of course. Fans and participants alike could also take part in the slew of silent auctions, continental breakfasts, autographing sessions, high teas and photo ops salted into the schedule.

"Our first official function is the kickoff banquet tonight," Dayna informed Mike. "That's when they'll draw for the initial pairings and course assignments."

She'd registered him as her personal guest, which would give him access to VIP seating at all events and, subsequently, to Dr. Wu. Along with the banquet ticket and laminated pass, she'd also prepared a thick binder.

"Mackenzie digitized the layouts for all five St. Andrews' courses. You can call up a three-dimensional topography of any hole, anytime, on your cell phone."

"Yeah, I took a look at the layouts during the flight from Algiers. They're pretty slick."

"They are, but I thought you might also want hard copies to study. They're easier on the eyes."

Particularly eyes showing a whole lot more red

than white. Hawk accepted the thick binder with heartfelt relief.

"Bless you, my child. I'll go through the schematics this afternoon. What's on your agenda until the banquet?"

"Wu Kim Li reserved a bay at the driving range at three o'clock. I snagged the one next to her at three-thirty. I figure it's as good a place as any to make the initial contact."

"Sounds like a plan. Do we need to do a comm check?"

"We should be good to go. Mac synchronized our emergency signals."

To demonstrate, Dayna pushed one of the knobs on the stainless steel chronometer banding her lift wrist and sent a silent jolt through the identical watch on Hawk's tanned wrist. Other knobs allowed the sophisticated devices to provide two-way communications or send data transmissions.

Assured their signals were in sync, Hawk hefted the binder and shoved out of his chair.

"I'll see you later. Good luck with Wu."

She'd need it, Dayna thought as she pulled on a butterscotch-colored windbreaker. Although late-May sunshine illuminated the wavy glass windows of her suite, she knew from previous experience that the breeze off St. Andrews Bay could slice like a barnacle. It could also wreak havoc with an otherwise perfect golf shot.

Zipping up the jacket, she collected her accessories. Field Dress had designed the slim, ultrachic fanny pack studded with Austrian crystals that clipped snuggly around her hip. One compartment holstered the sleek little Kahr PM40 micro-compact double-action pistol she'd cleared through British security. Others housed a spare ammo clip, her ID and credit cards and a tube of lip-gloss. A matching ball cap also studded with crystals shaded her face and contained her hair in a loose ponytail.

With her golf bag slung over her shoulder, Dayna left her two-room suite and walked to the elevators. After today she'd leave her equipment at the clubhouse storage facility for cleaning and repair. For now, its weight settled over her shoulder like an old familiar harness.

Although the hotel was a local landmark and one of the oldest in St. Andrews, it had been well maintained and modernized over the years. The elevator that ferried Dayna down four floors did so with quiet efficiency.

The lobby was a masterpiece of Victorian grandeur. High ceilings and dark paneling provided the perfect backdrop for red-tufted settees and antique sporting prints. A smoking room, book-lined library and glassed-in conservatory allowed guests to mix and mingle in the public rooms.

And mingle they did. Women dominated the milling crowd. Female corporate execs, commercial airline pilots, TV personalities, even a member of the Danish parliament—all had jumped at the chance to play with the great women golfers from around the world.

A good number of sportscasters and TV crews were also present, conducting impromptu interviews prior to tomorrow's official media day. They'd come armed with the printed list of participants and pounced on the Olympic gold medalist the moment she appeared.

"Dayna! Dayna! Over here!"

She gave two interviews, greeted a number of friends and acquaintances and autographed a program for one of the bellmen before finally making it to the hotel entrance.

The view through the revolving glass door was enough to take any golfer's breath away. Directly across the cobbled street lay the undulating fairways, man-eating gorse and killer sand traps of the fabled Old Course, known throughout the world as the Home of Golf. The gray granite bulk of the Royal and Ancient Golf Club ruled over the first tee with majestic splendor. Both course and clubhouse were framed by the salt marshes and sparkling waters of St. Andrews Bay.

Her gaze fixed on the panoramic vista, Dayna pushed through the revolving door and inadvertently plowed into a group of passersby.

"Excuse me. I wasn't looking…"

The rest of the apology stuck in her throat.

Well, hell! Her first day in St. Andrews and she had to run smack into the one man she'd hoped to avoid.

"Dayna! I'll be damned."

An all-too-familiar grin hiked up the corners of his mouth. Before she realized his intent, he hooked an arm around her waist and swooped in for a kiss.

His mouth covered hers, and for an instant, for one searing instant, the years rolled back. She was in college again. So hungry for this man she couldn't get enough of him, in or out of bed. So much in love she wanted the whole world to share her joy.

Reality returned with a crash. Remembering the bitterness that had followed her joy, Dayna jerked out of Luke Harper's arms.

Chapter 2

She was even more vibrant than he remembered.

The realization slammed into Luke as the woman he'd once thought he'd spend the rest of his life with backed away from him.

Her face was thinner than in their college days, her honey-colored hair lighter than he remembered. But her skin still had that healthy glow that came from regular exercise and hours spent outdoors while her eyes…

Christ, those eyes! How many times had Luke lost himself in their shimmering green depths? They'd been filled with such love and laughter then.

They weren't now. Flashing from fury to disdain in a single heartbeat, they raked him from head to toe.

"Harper."

That was it. No "Hey, Luke. Been a long time. Hope you finally got your head screwed on semistraight."

"Hello, Pud."

The pet name sent red flags into her cheeks, but before she could slice into him for using it, one of his buddies jabbed him in the ribs.

"Jeez, Harper, introduce us. Not that you need any introduction, Ms. Duncan." Elbowing Luke aside, the lanky American thrust out his hand. "I was on leave in Athens during the last Olympics and saw you paddle across the finish line for gold. The name's Alan. Alan Parks."

She shook his hand and relaxed into a smile, looking so much like the woman Luke had fallen for that his stomach pitched into a ninety-degree roll.

"These clowns," Parks said, "are Gabe, Tucker and Dweeb."

"Dweeb?"

"His call sign. Short for dumb-ass dweeber, after he missed a direct approach to a well-lit runway at a location that shall remain nameless."

"So you're all flyboys?"

"We are," Parks confirmed. "We're on an exchange tour, attached to RAF Leuchars."

sounded authentic even to their ears.

"We saw some of the advance PR on TV about the women's Pro-Am International," Parks said, eyeing her golf bag. "I didn't know you were competing in it, though."

"I'm a last-minute entrant. And I'd better hustle over to the driving range if I want to make it past the qualifying round. Nice meeting you all."

When she turned to Luke, all he got was a cool nod. He should have let it go with that. Like a fool, he didn't.

"Good to see you, Dayna."

"Sorry I can't say the same."

She walked off without a backward glance, leaving a stone-cold silence in her wake. Dweeb broke it with a low whistle.

"Damn, Harper. What did you do to the woman?"

Parks jumped in with a reply. "You haven't heard the story? Dayna Duncan and our boy here used to get all hot and heavy."

"No kidding?" Eyes wide, Dweeb followed her progress as she crossed the cobbled street. "What happened?"

"Woman got smart and dumped him. Best I recall, it happened a few months before the 2004 Olympics. That right, Harper?"

Luke didn't bother to correct him.

Like a radar lock, his gaze stayed fixed on Dayna's hip-swinging stride, trim rear and long legs. All the while his mind churned up memories of how those legs used to hook around his.

They'd met during the last half of his senior year at the University of Colorado. Luke was in air force ROTC and had been selected for pilot training. Dayna was a junior. A star athlete in both golf and kayaking, she was already a prime contender for the Olympic kayaking team.

They'd dated throughout the spring and into the summer, while Luke waited for an undergraduate pilot training slot to open up. Just the memory of those long, hot days and even hotter nights had him sweating under his leather bomber jacket.

Dayna began her senior year about the time Luke left for pilot training at Columbus AFB, Mississippi. They continued a long-distance love affair through-out the fall and into the winter—until Dayna's coach contacted Luke and bluntly informed him that she stood to lose both her scholarships and her spot on the Olympic team if she didn't cut out the cross-country commuting and focus.

Luke knew how desperately she wanted to make the team. He also knew he was about to enter the most intensive phase of pilot training. Following his head instead of his heart, he suggested they take a break. Hurt and angry, Dayna suggested *he* take a flying leap.

Judging by the acid dripping from her voice a few moments ago, she obviously thought he hadn't fallen far enough or hit anywhere near hard enough.

With a spear of regret for what they might have had, Luke thrust his hands in the pockets of his jacket and turned away.

"I need to head back to the base," he told his buddies. "I've got mission prebrief in a couple hours."

More rattled than she wanted to admit by the encounter, Dayna stalked past the Old Course's eighteenth green. Workmen were busy erecting bleachers and scaffolding for camera crews, but she barely noticed these modern scars on the face of the ancient course.

She'd known Luke Harper was stationed at the RAF base, dammit. She should have been more prepared for a chance meeting with her old flame.

That was as good a description as any for him, Dayna thought with a stab of self-disgust. She'd gone off the deep end, but Luke Harper had never loved her. Lusted for her, yes. Driven her half out of her mind with his muscular body and his busy, busy hands, certainly. Yet he'd cut the cord fast enough

Something to remember, she told herself fiercely as she hailed a shuttle. The gaily decorated carts ferried golfers between the five courses, two clubhouses, modern golf academy and state-of-the-art practice center that comprised the St. Andrews Links complex.

"G'day to ye, Ms. Duncan." The trolley driver greeted her with the rolling Scots burr that required careful attention by the listener or the services of an interpreter. "Are ye gaein' oot for a bit o' practice?"

"Yes, I am. Would you take me to the driving range, please."

"I wud indeed." Relieving her of her bag, he stowed it on the rack at the rear of the cart. "Off we go, then."

Dayna used the short drive and the stiff breeze coming in off the bay to blow Luke Harper out of her head. The man was history. For the next week her sole focus would be Wu Kim Li.

Kim Li *and* this course, she thought, eyeing the rolling fairways and deep sand traps. It was the oldest course in Scotland, the playground of kings and commoners, covering a stretch of land beside the sea like an old, crumpled carpet. Unlike the manicured fairways and lushly landscaped grounds of most U.S. courses, St. Andrews pitted man against the elements. There were no stands of pine or oak to blunt the often gale-force winds that blew in from the bay, no banks of colorful azalea or rhododendrons to separate the holes.

The fairways had been planted centuries ago in a stubby, scruffy native grass that put its roots deep into the sandy soil and sent shock waves through wrists and arms when hit with a club at the wrong angle. Worse, there wasn't a level patch anywhere on the course. The burns, sways, gorse-topped hummocks and treacherous sand traps required intense concentration on every shot. Dayna would have a real challenge to keep her ball in play and Wu Kim Li in her sights.

She found the North Korean holding court at the practice center.

A modern facility devoted to the art and science of golf, the center's driving range boasted sixty bays with air-cushioned mats and automated power tees. Wu Kim Li occupied the center bay—in full view of television crews crammed into the glassed-in viewing area, naturally.

By shamelessly playing on her name and former Olympic glory, Dayna had snagged the bay next to the teenaged megastar. She waited patiently until the golfer who had it before her finished, then walked out to the open-sided booth. Removing the head cover of her back and did a few stretching exercises.

The movement snagged the attention of a woman two stalls down. Obviously an amateur, the observer violated range etiquette by calling an excited greeting.

"Hi, Dayna! I'm Ann Foster. I saw you were registered for this tournament. Hope we get to play together."

Reluctant to disturb the others' concentration, Dayna merely smiled and tipped her club in response. The golfer in the next bay, however, wasn't nearly as restrained.

"*Tak-cho!*" Wu Kim Li followed her disgusted exclamation with an immediate translation. "That mean be quiet. We practice here."

Kim Li turned her back on the now thoroughly embarrassed amateur. Eyes narrow, she raked Dayna from the brim of her ball cap to her soft-spike shoes. She was sizing up the competition obviously, or trying to pysch her out.

No stranger to the guerilla warfare of sports, Dayna teed up a ball and swung. Her driver connected with a solid whap. The ball soared in a high, smooth arc. With another loud crack, it bounced off the metal sign designating the two-hundred-and-fifty-yards mark.

Not bad for a first practice shot. Not bad at all— unless, of course, you were trying to worm your way into the good graces of a rival sports star like Wu Kim Li.

Dayna could feel the competitive vibes eddying across the stall as the North Korean addressed her ball. With a whoosh, Wu's driver sliced through the air.

Two seventy.

Dayna teed up, swung again.

Two seventy-five.

Wu's driver descended, connected.

Three hundred, or close enough to generate an outburst of spontaneous applause from the women who'd interrupted their practice to watch the impromptu competition. Wu accepted the ovation as her due and unbent enough to offer Dayna a grudging compliment.

"Your swing very good."

"Not as good as yours."

"I young," Wu said with a careless shrug. "Have more strength."

Yeah, right. Dayna would love to plunk the little twerp into a kayak, drop her in Alberta's Castle River during the spring runoff and let her see what kind of strength it took to finish the course.

Trying her damnedest to sound friendly, she teed up another ball. "They draw for the initial pairings at the banquet tonight. Maybe we'll play together."

Wu turned away with another shrug.

* * *

The kickoff banquet was held at the venerable Royal and Ancient Golf Clubhouse.

Showered, shaved and looking ruggedly handsome in tan slacks and a navy blazer with an embroidered Military Marksmanship Association patch on its pocket, Mike escorted Dayna into a banquet hall lavish with eighteenth-century crown moldings and intricately patterned parquet floors. Tables laden with glowing candles and sparkling crystal added to the elegant atmosphere. The waiters wore tuxedos, the women were in cocktail dresses and many of the Scottish tournament officials sported kilts. The talk, however, was all sports.

Dayna introduced Mike to some of the greats in women's golf, many of whom said graciously that they hoped to draw her for a partner. She also met a number of the amateurs who, like her, had interrupted busy professional lives to play in this charity tournament. All the while she and Mike kept steering toward their targets.

"There they are," Dayna murmured, indicating the Wus with a small nod.

The Koreans stood in the middle of a swarm of TV execs and tournament officials. The group also included Kim Li's support team—her manager, her trainer, her agent, her PR rep, her bodyguards. Every one of them, Dayna knew, charged with ensuring that North Korea's darling and her father returned home after the tournament.

Kim Li spotted their approach and summoned them into her royal presence with a lift of her chin. Her dark eyes were all over Mike as Dayna made the intros.

"This is my friend, Mike Callahan."

"This my father, Dr. Wu Xia-Dong."

Both Mike and Dayna shook the scientist's hand. She didn't need more than a touch of Wu's clammy palm to sense his nervousness.

"You must be very proud of your daughter."

The flicker of acknowledgment in his eyes told Dayna he'd understood the compliment, but he waited to respond until a North Korean with a badge that identified him as an official interpreter had murmured in his ear.

"So sorry. My English very bad." Wu turned a smile on his daughter. "Kim Li make all Korea proud."

The girl returned it with the first genuine warmth Dayna had seen on her face. Whatever else the teen had going on in her life, she obviously loved her dad.

They couldn't have spent much time together. The detailed dossier OMEGA had assembled on the Wus indicated Kim Li had lived at a government-sponsored athletic training center for thirteen of her eighteen years. Dr. Wu's work had kept him isolated at the center of a small, highly select cadre of scientists. Kim Li's mother was the one who'd made periodic visits to the training center until her death a few years ago. Yet the bond between father and daughter seemed as strong and unshakable as the report had suggested.

Any defection would definitely have to be a package deal.

That thought stayed with Dayna throughout the banquet and the pairings that followed. By the luck of the draw, she was teamed with Eleanor Tolbert. A longtime member of the Ladies Professional Golf Association, Eleanor was one of its biggest money-winners. She and Dayna would have been the team to beat in scratch golf, but this was a charity event so handicaps were used to level the playing field. The ranker the amateur, the higher her handicap and the more strokes deducted from her final score.

Wu Kim Li drew one of those high-handicapped amateurs for her partner. An Irish neurosurgeon, as it turned out, with little time for golf but a wild enthusiasm for the sport. Flame-haired Brianna Kilkenny towered over her partner during the media barrage that followed the drawing. Unwilling to stand in anyone's shadow, Wu adroitly sidestepped and took the cameras with her.

To Dayna's intense satisfaction, the links draw

put her and Eleanor on the same course as Kim Li and her partner for the initial qualifying rounds. They weren't in the same foursome and would tee off at different times, but she would make opportunities to connect with the girl while Mike worked the father.

The two agents reconvened in Dayna's suite after the banquet.

A cold, damp fog had rolled in off the bay. Rather than up the room's thermostat, Dayna put a match to the kindling laid in the brick-and-tile fireplace. The neatly stacked logs soon caught the flames. Snapping and crackling, they filled the sitting room with a pine-resin scent.

Mike had studied the course layouts Dayna had given him earlier that afternoon. He'd also annotated a detailed map of the St. Andrews area. Together, they went over emergency escape routes and formulated options for detaching Wu and his daughter from their watchdogs.

"Assuming they really want to defect."

"Yeah," Mike agreed. "Big assumption. We've got the next week to find out if it's true."

"If it is, I don't think Kim Li will want to pull a disappearing act until after the tournament. She's too competitive."

"That's my assessment, too. We can move sooner

if we have to, but for now we'll plan to whisk her and her Papa Wu away immediately following the trophy presentation. We'll use the crowd and the media to run interference with their handlers. I've coordinated with our counterparts in the CIA and British Intelligence. They'll provide back-up, transport vehicles and escort to our departure point."

He thumped a knuckle against the air base just northwest of the town of St. Andrews proper.

"One of the crews from the USAF detachment at RAF Leuchars will fly us back to the States. I figure I'd head over there before your practice round tomorrow and bring the detachment commander up to speed."

Dayna hesitated. She hated to introduce the subject of her failed romance, but Hawk needed to know it might present a complication.

"Before you talk to the detachment commander, you should be aware that I used to date one of his pilots. Captain Luke Harper."

Mike cut her a surprised look. "I remember the hype about you and some flyboy. He's here, at Leuchars?"

"He is. Matter of fact, I bumped into him this afternoon."

Bumped, as in locked lips. To Dayna's profound disgust, the memory of Luke's mouth on hers sent heat seeping into her cheeks. She fought to keep her expression neutral but Hawkeye hadn't earned his code name by missing subtle signals. Nor had he stayed alive as long as he had in this business by shrugging off even small, seemingly innocuous incidents as mere coincidence.

"Are you sure it was a chance meeting?"

Like Hawk, Dayna had learned the hard way that training and experience were no substitutes for gut instinct. She went with hers now.

"I'm sure. I was a last-minute entry in this tournament. Harper didn't know I was coming to St. Andrews and he doesn't have a clue I work for the government. The problem is, he isn't supposed to be here, either."

When she indicated he flew the super-secret Stealth bomber, Hawk grasped the implications immediately. The material he'd studied on the flight up from Algiers had included a brief detailing of the antiwar movements in Britain and the sensitive issue of the presence of U.S. nuclear-capable bombers on British soil.

"If the media gloms on to his presence and tries to resurrect your old affair, it could jeopardize both his mission and ours."

"Lightning and I discussed that," Dayna replied. "Our initial assessment was that the air force has sufficient measures in place to keep their operation at Leuchars under wraps, but…"

She blew out a long breath. The unexpected encounter this afternoon had forced her to reevaluate the situation. St. Andrews was a small university town, crammed at present with newshounds from around the world. Any one of them could sniff out the story of her old flame.

"You'd better lay out the problem when you meet with the detachment commander in the morning," she told Hawk. "Get his take on the threat to his operation."

"Will do." Those too-keen eyes studied hers. "What about the threat to ours?"

"I've been thinking about that, too. If the media does latch on to my old romance, we *could* use the hype to deflect attention from our efforts to get close to the Wus."

"Something to consider," Hawk agreed, "but you don't sound too thrilled about letting this character back in your life. Just say the word and I'll take him out of the picture."

Lightning had already made that offer. Once again, Dayna turned it down.

"No need. The meeting this afternoon caught me by surprise. I'll be prepared if it happens again."

She was still trying to convince herself of that some four hours later.

Lifting her head, Dayna glared at the digital alarm

beside her bed. When she saw the hour, she let loose with an expletive that would have earned her a warning if she'd muttered it during the tournament. Still swearing, she dropped her face into the goose-down pillow.

This was ridiculous. She was playing a double game of golf and deception tomorrow. She'd have to make every stroke count while keeping tabs on Wu Kim Li. She needed sleep.

"Get out of my head, Harper!"

Chapter 3

Why couldn't he put the woman out of his head?

Luke shifted restlessly in the mission commander's seat of his bat-winged B-2. The pilot whose performance he'd been evaluating occupied the left seat, breathing easier now that he'd completed most of his check ride.

Outside the cockpit a star-studded night sky stretched to infinity. Inside, the instrument panel gave off a muted glow shielded by specially screened and darkened windows.

"Thirty-two thousand and holding steady on course niner-three-six," the other pilot reported.

Luke acknowledged their position and rolled his shoulders to relieve the strain of his seat harness. They'd been in the air for seven hours now, a mere hop compared to their normal missions. Tonight's training run had taken them out over the Atlantic for an in-flight refueling. They would return to base before dawn, gliding in with the same stealth that made the B-2 invisible to the world's most sophisticated radars—and to antiwar protestors hoping to obtain photos that would prove beyond any doubt the bomber's presence in the U.K.

The B-2 crews and support personnel were every bit as determined to remain as stealthy as the two-billion-dollar aircraft they flew. Hence the night-only takeoffs and landings and the fiction that their detachment was part of an exchange program at Leuchars.

So far the ploy had worked. Would it still work if the paparazzi sniffed out the fact that Dayna Duncan's old flame just happened to be in St. Andrews?

From past experience, Luke knew how the media rooted around for personal tidbits to salt into their coverage of otherwise impersonal sporting events. He and Pud had once provided just the mix of glamour and romance the tabloids loved.

The nickname tugged his mouth into a lopsided grin. Pud, short for the puddles he'd teased her about paddling around in. The teasing had lasted only until she'd taken Luke for his first white-water run.

The experience had been as exhilarating as any he'd every experienced. It had also scared the crap out of him. When they'd gone over Horseshoe Falls, his stomach had dropped right through the bottom of the fiberglass kayak. He could still hear Dayna's joyous whoop, still see her hair flying under her helmet and wet suit molded to her curves as they…

Well, hell! There she was again. Front and center in his thoughts.

Resigned, Luke checked the instruments and gave up trying to shove the woman out of his head.

She was still there, hovering around the edges of his mind, when he finished his mission debrief. Slinging his flyaway bag over his shoulder, he exited the debriefing area and was headed for the crew room to change out of his flight suit when one of other pilots hailed him.

"The old man wants to see you, Harper."

Nodding, Luke detoured to the suite of offices tucked in one corner of the massive hangar. He figured the colonel was waiting for an update on the check ride just completed and prepared a rundown in his mind.

"You wanted to see me, sir?"

Colonel Don Anderson waved him into the office. Big, barrel-chested and as strong as a Brahma bull, Anderson had been part of the initial B-2 cadre. In the decade since, he'd racked up more hours than most pilots did in a lifetime. Customarily gruff and to the point, Anderson jerked his chin at the stranger seated in the chair angled in front of his desk.

"Harper, this is Mike Callahan. He's with the government. Callahan, Captain Luke Harper."

The stranger rose and offered his hand. His square-shouldered bearing suggested he'd spent at least one hitch in the military. The embroidered sharpshooter's patch plainly visible above his visitor's badge indicated he wasn't someone to mess with.

"Harper."

Callahan's grip stopped well short of bone-crunching but something in the man's narrow-eyed, assessing look stirred an instinctive and wholly atavistic response in Luke. Without warning, the skin on the back of his neck prickled.

"Callahan's got all the necessary security clearances," Anderson said. "I want you to show him our operation. Bring him back here when you're done."

"Yes, sir."

Wondering what this was all about, Luke stashed his flyaway bag with the colonel's exec and walked Callahan toward the hangar bay.

"I don't know how much the colonel told you about our detachment—"

"He indicated you're one of several recently established forward operating locations. Before that, B-2 crews flew combat missions from your home base at Whiteman AFB, Missouri. Must have made for a helluva long haul."

"It did," Luke admitted. "It also made for a surreal life. A pilot could roll out of bed, kiss his wife goodbye, fly a thirty- to forty-hour combat mission against heavily defended targets halfway around the world and return home in time to take out the trash the next morning. Even with forward basing, we spend a lot of time in the air."

Callahan's glance dropped. "I don't see a ring. No one to kiss goodbye in the morning?"

"No one special," Luke replied, ruthlessly suppressing the image that leaped into his head of a laughing, loving Dayna. He'd had his chance with her and blown it. It was just his own tough luck he hadn't found anyone else in the years since.

"So how long does it take to prepare for one of these marathon missions?" Callahan asked.

"If we're lucky, we get three or four days advance notice. That gives us time to study the target, plan our ingress and egress routes and adjust our sleep and eating patterns to maximize our alertness in flight."

"I can see sleep, but eating?"

"The air force shelled out big bucks to dieticians to determine optimal liquid intake and the best ratio of carbs versus protein to sustain long periods of activity." Luke had to grin. "All those experts finally concluded we'd found an optimal mix in our traditional bomber dogs. Hot dogs doused in chili," he explained. "We warm them in the cockpit heater."

Shouldering open a door, he led the way into one of the two cavernous hangars the Brits had turned over to the B-2 detachment. The aircraft Luke had just flown occupied center court, being serviced by the ground crews.

"Our birds remain undercover at all times while on the ground. We want to keep their advanced design and special 'low-observable' characteristics away from prying eyes. In flight, they're damned near invisible. Pretty slick, aren't they?"

And then some! Mike Callahan had jumped out of plenty of planes during his stint as an army Ranger but he'd never seen anything as lethal as these black boomerangs. They were immense, with a wingspan of at least a hundred-and-fifty feet, yet their flat fuselage and long, sloping cockpits made them appear saucer-thin from the side. The darkened cockpit windows seemed to follow the two men like a predator's eyes as Harper led the way across a hangar floor painted and buffed to a bright sheen.

"The B-2's unique bat-wing shape and the special coating used on its skin are designed to deflect radar waves." Harper slapped a hand against the cowling of one of the four powerful engines. "And these babies are so quiet they wouldn't wake your grandma from her afternoon nap if we flew over her house at a hundred feet."

A slight exaggeration, Callahan guessed wryly, although Harper's description of how the engines dispensed their exhaust across the top of the wings to shield the aircraft from heat-seeking missiles below brought the seriousness of its mission into sharp focus.

As he listened to the pilot explain the details of his unit's operation, Mike assessed the man behind the uniform. Rogue had stated unequivocally that any feelings she'd once harbored for Harper had died years ago. She was also confident that his presence at RAF Leuchars wouldn't throw her off her game. Mike trusted her judgment on that. Like him, she'd competed in countless nerve-bending competitions. She knew better than anyone else what would—or wouldn't—impact her performance.

The question that now had to be answered was whether *her* presence would impact Harper's mission if the press IDed him as Dayna's former lover and came sniffing around the captain. Mike had discussed the situation with his commander when they'd met earlier. The more he saw of the B-2 operation, the more he agreed with the colonel's decision to take drastic measures to shield the detachment from prying eyes.

From the pride in Harper's voice as he described his bird and its mission, Mike guessed the pilot was *not* going to like those measures.

That became instantly apparent when the two men returned to the colonel's office. Responding to Mike's subtle nod, Anderson dropped the ax.

"I told you Callahan here works for the government. His sources told *him* that you once had a romantic relationship with one of the golfers competing in the Women's International Pro-Am Charity Golf Tournament at St. Andrews."

Harper was quick. Surprise blanked his face for mere seconds before giving way to wary comprehension.

"That's right. Dayna Duncan. I didn't realize our one-time relationship was a matter of government interest."

Harper leveled a hard stare in Mike's direction before turning back to the colonel.

"I can see the complications to our detachment's mission," he conceded reluctantly. "Someone in the media is bound to recognize me and start snooping around to find out why I'm in the U.K."

Anderson didn't waste words. "Then you'll understand why I've arranged to have you reassigned to the 3rd AF Executive Support Unit, with detached duty here at RAF Leuchars, effective immediately."

"What?"

"You'll act as liaison with the British VIP support section across base. That way, if asked, you can say with absolute honesty that you're attached to the RAF unit. You're still current on the C-21 Learjet, which is one of the aircraft they use to transport VIPs, so it shouldn't be a difficult transition."

"To hell with difficult!"

Harper's disgust at being relegated to the status of a flying cabdriver overcame his ingrained respect for authority and rank.

"I'm scheduled for a run over a heavily defended target in two days and you're going to pull me to haul VIPs around the capitals of Europe?"

Anderson hadn't earned his eagles without learning how to use them. Even Mike felt the ice when the colonel leaned forward.

"I'm well aware of the schedule, Captain, and yes, I'm pulling you."

Harper clamped his mouth shut over further protests but a muscle ticked in the side of his jaw.

"Since you've just come off a mission, I want you to take twenty-four hours to decompress. Report to the Brits' Executive Support Section tomorrow morning. They'll have a desk waiting for you."

An expression of acute pain crossed the pilot's face. "A desk," he muttered under his breath.

Anderson wasn't much happier about losing one of his best pilots, but he tried to soften the blow.

"Sorry we have to go this route, Luke. You know the security of our unit has to come first."

"Yes, sir."

"That's all."

Dismissed, the pilot speared Hawk with an angry look and departed.

"Damn," Anderson muttered when Harper had cleared the room. "I hate to lose him, even temporarily. He's one of our best." His glance was almost as disgusted as Harper's. "I want him back as soon as you complete your mission. Make sure everyone in your chain of command understands that."

"Will do."

Hawk contacted Dayna as soon as he was clear of the base. Although dawn was just beginning to break, he knew she'd be up and preparing for her practice round. Succinctly, he briefed her on Luke Harper's change in status.

"It didn't sit well with him."

"Tough."

Hawk hesitated. His loyalty lay with Rogue and the other OMEGA operatives, first, last and always. Yet Luke Harper had impressed him with both his expertise and his obvious dedication to his mission.

"Harper knows this area and the base, Rogue. Might be some way we could exploit that knowledge."

The suggestion was met with thunderous silence.

"Just something to think about. I'll brief Lightning on my visit. You go give 'em hell on the links."

Some miles ahead, Luke steered through the outskirts of town, still simmering.

The United States was at war with an army of fanatical terrorists, for God's sake! U.S. troops took hits daily in hot spots around the world. Every crew dog worth his or her salt wanted to help bring the war to a swift and decisive end. Thanks to his long-ago romance with Dayna Duncan, Luke's contribution to the effort would now involve ferrying military and civilian bigwigs around Europe. What a waste of his years of training and experience!

But the security of his unit came first. It would always come first. Acceptance of that unequivocal fact took the edge from Luke's anger and disgust as turned onto the street leading to his rented flat.

The sight of the TV vans crowding the entrance to his apartment building sent his stomach into a ninety-degree pitch. How had they nosed him out so quickly?

He got the answer when he parked and exited his car amid a swarm of reporters and one of them shoved an early-morning paper in his face.

"Is this you, Captain Harper?"

He could hardly deny the evidence two inches from his nose. There he was, right on the front page, with his arm wrapped around Dayna's waist and his mouth covering hers. While Luke studied the photo, the questions exploded all around him.

"What's the story with you and Dayna Duncan?"

"Are you two picking up where you left off?"

"How long have you been stationed in Scotland?"

"Did Dayna sign up for this tournament so you two could reconnect?"

"Will you be in the gallery to watch her practice round?"

Luke thought fast. The damage was done. If he brushed aside their questions, these bloodhounds would dig until they came up with a story. The only solution he could see at this point was to brazen it out and give them enough juicy copy to satisfy even their voracious appetites.

With a dart of savage satisfaction, he set the stage. "Sure, I'll be there to see her play."

"She tees off at nine," another reporter warned after a quick check of his watch.

The perfect exit line, Luke thought as he inserted his key in the door lock. "Guess we'd all better hustle."

It took Dayna three tries before she finally escaped the media frenzy spawned by the photo in the morning paper. Even then reporters trailed her and her partner, Eleanor Tolbert, out of the clubhouse with cameras rolling.

The wind knifed off the bay, making Dayna glad she'd opted for weatherproof microfiber pants and jacket in eye-popping red. The stiff breeze covered the apology she murmured to Eleanor.

"Sorry 'bout all that hoopla."

"It doesn't bother me if it doesn't bother you," the longtime LPGA star said with a smile. "Hel-lo. What's this?"

This, Dayna discovered, was Wu Kim Li busily signing autographs for her hordes of fans.

The North Korean and her partner had drawn a later time slot and weren't scheduled to tee off for another half hour. If the teen had any regard for links etiquette, she would have delayed her arrival on the course or waited in the clubhouse until called to the tee box. Naturally, such minor considerations as common courtesy and fair play couldn't be expected to keep her from the fawning adoration of her fans.

Wu glanced up as Dayna and Eleanor emerged, trailed by the string of reporters. Abruptly, she shoved the autograph book into the hands of a fan and strolled over to shake hands with her competitors. That was the excuse she gave for getting her face in front of the cameras, anyway.

"I wish you good practice round."

"Thanks," Eleanor returned. "Same to you."

Wu nodded and turned to Dayna. "I see picture of you with boyfriend."

"Ex-boyfriend."

"Boyfriend, *ex*-boyfriend, no difference." Oozing false sympathy, the teen clucked her tongue. "Both bad for concentration."

Yeah, right! Nothing like a little psychological warfare designed to throw your opponent off her game.

"You think?"

"I know. I have many boyfriends."

Sternly, Dayna reminded herself that she was there to cozy up to the girl, not spar with her.

"Maybe we should get together later and compare notes," she suggested.

Wu's shrug couldn't have conveyed less interest. Without another word, she strolled back to her fans. Eleanor was too seasoned a pro to comment on the exchange, but the look she sent her partner as they walked to the tee box spoke volumes.

All of which Dayna could have put out of her head if she hadn't skimmed a glance around the gallery and spotted Luke Harper.

She could hardly miss him. The man had as many cameras aimed in his direction as Dayna did in hers. All too aware that they'd captured her in midgawk, she responded to Luke's two-fingered salute with a smile that came up just short of friendly.

Dammit! What was he doing here?

Hawk had indicated Harper wasn't happy about his abrupt change in status. Did Luke think Dayna had engineered the move? Was he planning to exact some form of revenge by following her around the course?

If so, he—and Wu Kim Li—had another think coming. Dayna had been forced to shut Luke Harper out of her head once before to win gold. She could— She *would* do the same today.

All she had to do was wait her turn. Step into the box. Tee up. Decide on her line of flight. Address the ball.

Focus.

The noisy crowd quieted. The TV cameras faded. The world diminished to a square patch of green-brown grass and a round white sphere.

Focus.

Her driver rose in a fluid backswing and exploded

downward. With a loud crack, the ball flew across a fairway humped with rolling burns and cut a corner of thick brown gorse. It landed dead center less than a hundred yards from the green to a chorus of whoops and shouts.

Dayna couldn't help herself. With a spear of fierce satisfaction, she angled her head until her glance locked with Luke's.

Take that, Harper!

Chapter 4

Dayna finished her first round at six under par—
without resorting to any of Mackenzie's special aids.

She left the course squinty-eyed from peering into
the stiff breeze that had whipped up the contents of
St. Andrews' notorious sand traps. Grit clogged
Dayna's pores and wild tendrils had escaped her
French braid to whip around her face and visor, but
she was so pumped from the game she wasn't worried about looking like a walking maypole. Slapping
on some lip-gloss, she joined Eleanor in front of the
cameras for the obligatory post-round news conference.

Her good mood slipped a little when she was forced to field more questions about Luke Harper than about her game. She kept her cool, however, and joined the other women in the lounge reserved for their exclusive use to watch the last few foursomes finish up.

"That girl's a machine," one of the pros commented as Wu Kim Li chipped onto the seventeenth green.

When Wu's ball rolled to within three inches of the cup, the gallery exploded. When her amateur partner chipped over the green and into the water, Wu looked as though *she* was going to explode. Her face a thundercloud, the North Korean stalked onto the green and holed out.

Mutters rolled around the lounge but none of the pros would dish a fellow golfer out loud. Dayna was too busy scanning the gallery for Wu's father to pay any attention to the buzz. She spotted the scientist standing at the ropes, shoulder to shoulder with two burly North Koreans. Hawk was also in the crowd just a few yards away.

Anxious to hear whether he'd made contact with the father, Dayna waited with mounting impatience for an opportunity to approach the daughter. It finally came an hour later, after Kim Li had finished her round and postured for the media. When she and her partner entered the lounge, the flame-haired Irish neurosurgeon peeled away from Wu and aimed for the bar. She didn't exude the air of someone who'd enjoyed her first pairing with a pro.

Dayna used that as her cue to head for the locker room. The intel OMEGA had provided indicated Kim Li held to a rigid post-game ritual that included a sauna, a shower and a massage to loosen the tension kinks. Her personal masseuse traveled with her as part of the support team.

The woman—yes, Dayna was sure she was female—had already set up her portable massage table and array of scented oils. Looking like a sumo wrestler in white polyester, she sported bulging muscles and a bulldog neck. Her knuckles rested gorilla-like on the table as she followed Dayna's progress through the locker area to the steam room.

Stripping, Dayna tucked a Turkish towel around her but delayed entering the sauna until she heard Kim Li come into the locker room and exchange a few words in Korean with the masseuse. Luckily, the only other occupant of the steam room exited just as Dayna went in. She had the lung-sucking heat all to herself until Kim Li joined her.

The girl nodded a greeting and dropped onto the opposite bench. Her towel puddled on the bench, baring her above the waist as she leaned back on her elbows. Her exhibitionist sprawl indicated a total lack of self-consciousness. It also let Dayna see the teen wasn't sporting any hidden listening or recording devices.

"You played good game," the Korean said after she'd settled herself comfortably.

The compliment was grudging at best. Dayna returned it with a smile. "So did you and Dr. Kilkenny."

"That one! Pah! Her swing is good, but short game needs practice. Much practice."

"That would require quite a trade-off, wouldn't it?"

"How do you mean, trade-off?"

"If she practiced as much as you suggest, she'd have to cut back on saving people's lives."

The sarcasm went right over Wu's head.

"Me, I give up much. You, too, I think, for your sport. Kilkenny want to play better, she must practice."

Good Lord! No wonder the neurosurgeon had aimed straight for the bar.

Deciding she'd better cut to the chase before they were interrupted, Dayna eased into the sensitive subject of defection. "I saw you play at Cypress Point."

"You watch me on TV?"

"Yes."

Several times. The videotape of the brief exchange on the eighteenth green was burned into Dayna's brain.

"You said something on the last green."

Kim Li didn't alter her unselfconscious sprawl, but a sudden, subtle tension infused the damp heat.

"You said you'd be here at St. Andrews," Dayna said. "You asked your partner to…"

The girl's sudden shift in focus cut her off. Dayna glanced left and saw the sumo wrestler's flat, broad face at the glass insert in the sauna's door. Her eyes narrowed to slits, the masseuse peered through the swirling steam.

She couldn't hear their conversation through the thick glass…unless *she* packed some kind of super-sensitive listening device. Probably not, or she wouldn't have advertised her presence at the door. Still, Dayna smothered a curse when Kim Li gathered her towel and draped it around her hips.

"I must go now. Time for massage."

"That's as far as I got," Dayna related to Hawk when they convened in her suite some hours later.

She'd traded her poppy-red wind suit for tailored gray slacks and a V-necked sweater in white cotton interwoven with shimmering gold thread. Raking a hand through her freshly washed and blow-dried hair, she made a face.

"Kim Li jumped up and scurried out the minute Big Mama showed her face."

"I didn't fare much better," Hawk admitted. "Dr. Wu's two escorts never strayed more than a few feet from his side. We did manage a few polite exchanges but nothing that gave any indication of whether he really wants to defect."

"We'll have to detach one or both from their bodyguards."

Frowning, Dayna studied the schedule for the remainder of the day. "There's an autographing at four, followed by a silent auction. I'll try to get Kim Li aside during one session or the other."

"In the meantime, I'll hit the lounge. Dr. Wu's background dossier says he's a Scotch drinker. I noticed he put away two stiff ones at the banquet last night. I figure he might respond to an invitation to sample some of Scotland's finest whiskeys from another aficionado."

Dayna had never seen Hawk down anything stronger than a beer. "Since when are you a connoisseur of Scotch whiskeys?"

"Since a half hour ago, when I got a crash course from the bartender downstairs. Would you believe they stock more than a hundred different labels? One costs almost fifty British pounds for a single shot."

"Good grief! A hundred dollars a whiff?"

"All in the line of duty." Grinning, Hawk pushed out of the easy chair. "I'll let you know later how it goes."

"Same here."

Dayna was already strategizing the autographing in her mind when her partner opened the door. He froze for a moment, putting her on instant alert, before making a brief announcement.

"You've got company."

Kim Li, she thought with a leap of excitement.

She hurried forward. Two skips later came to dead stop. Luke stood in the hall with his feet planted wide and a distinctly unfriendly expression on his face. When his glance cut from Hawk to Dayna, it didn't get any friendlier.

"So you and Callahan know each other."

"Obviously," she returned. "Not that it's any of your business."

"The hell it isn't."

He started into the room. Hawk blocked his entry with one sidestep.

"I'm not feeling real sociable right now," Luke warned. "You might want to get out of my way."

"And you might want to rethink your tone."

Hawk's drawled reply ratcheted up both the tension and the testosterone. Dayna figured she'd better wade in before blood flowed.

"It's okay, Mike. Let him in."

Hawk stood aside. After surveying the suite with a narrow glance, Luke brought his gaze back to Dayna.

"Cozy," he commented, obviously thinking she shared the suite with Hawk. She didn't disabuse him.

"What do you want, Harper?"

"An explanation, for starters. It appears we have a mutual acquaintance in Mr. Callahan here. What's your connection to him?"

Irritated by both his tone and his presence, Dayna struggled to put her personal animosity aside.

Hawk had already relayed his opinion regarding Harper to her and to Lightning. OMEGA's director had given the green light to use the pilot's expertise if necessary. Dayna wasn't ready to include Luke, but she knew she had to feed him sufficient information to keep him from complicating the sensitive op more than he already had.

"Mike and I work together on special projects for the government. You don't need to know the specific project that brought us to St. Andrews. Suffice to say, your detachment's presence at RAF Leuchars was a complication we had to deal with. We couldn't take the chance that…"

"So you got me transferred out of my unit," he interrupted, his hazel eyes as hard as granite.

"Yes, but…"

"Do you have any appreciation of the impact my abrupt move will have on the other pilots? Guys like Dweeb and Gabe and Alan Parks?"

"I have a general idea."

"And it doesn't bother you that you've just doubled their cockpit hours, not to mention their exposure to the surface-to-air missiles surrounding the targets we go after?"

Dayna could count on the fingers of one hand the number of men she'd allowed to get this close *or* this hostile.

"Back off, Harper! I have my orders. You have yours."

"Yeah, well, I suggest you give me a little more detail on just what your orders entail so I don't blow it the next time a reporter shoves a mike at me."

"I've told you all you need to know."

"Wrong."

"Don't push me, Harper. I can't think of anything I would enjoy more than seriously rearranging your pretty face."

A sardonic glint worked its way through Luke's bristling antagonism. "Seems I recall you wanting to rearrange more than my pretty face, Pud."

"Don't call me that!"

"You used to like it."

"I *used* to like a lot of things. That includes you."

She regretted the childish retort as soon as it was out. They both had too much at stake to indulge in this kind of petty sniping. Disgusted with herself, she turned to Hawk.

"Sorry. You didn't need to hear us slinging around this old baggage."

"We all collect baggage."

His quiet admission acted like a sprinkler system on the firestorm of emotions Luke had churned up. Dayna had worked a number of ops with Mike Callahan yet knew so little about the man behind the marksmanship badge. He never talked about his past and she knew better than to ask.

She'd heard rumors about a woman. A DEA agent who'd died in a firefight deep in the jungles of Colombia. Some said she'd gone bad. Some said Hawk had been sent in to uncover the truth. If so, whatever had happened in that steamy green darkness would go to the grave with him.

Unless Gillian Ridgeway pried it out of him. Dayna wouldn't bet on that happening. Then again, Jilly *was* the daughter of two of OMEGA's most skilled operatives.

Callahan could handle that problem when and if it ever arose. He—and Dayna—had other issues to tackle right now. One of which was standing a few feet away.

"I know you don't want to hear this," Hawk said, breaking into her thoughts, "but Captain Harper has a point. After that photo this morning, the media is going to be on him like crows on road kill."

"They already are," she admitted. "He had as many cameras aimed in his direction out on the course as I did."

"Then you need to hammer out a coordinated response to the barrage you know is going to follow." His glance cut from Dayna to Luke and back again. "I'll let you decide how much to tell him. Brief me when you're through."

When the door closed behind him, Dayna's mouth settled into a thin line. Damned if Luke Harper hadn't wormed his way back into her life.

Temporarily.

He'd be out again as soon as she hustled Wu Kim Li and her father onto a plane. With that thought firmly in mind, she forced a show of civility.

"Would you like a drink?"

The stiff set to his shoulders relaxed a little. "Sounds good."

"Beer, wine or something stronger?"

"A beer's fine."

She could do this, Dayna told herself as she crossed to the well-stocked minibar and removed two bottles of ale from the fridge. She could bury the past, forget how hungry she'd once been for this man, stay focused on the job ahead.

"Here, let me do that."

Taking the bottles from her hand, he twisted off the caps and passed one back. His eyes held hers as he offered a neutral toast.

"Here's to another round like the one you shot this morning."

When they clinked bottles and he tipped his to his mouth, the past crashed right through Dayna's firm resolve to remain in the present.

Her ale halted halfway to her lips. With a sudden wrenching in her belly, she watched the smooth play of muscle and tendon as Luke took a long swallow.

Oh, God! How many times had she nuzzled that warm niche just under his chin? How often had she licked her way up, then down the strong column of his throat? And how many times had she kicked herself for falling for someone who could put her out of his life so easily?

Never again, she vowed fiercely as she downed the dark, fruity ale.

Chapter 5

What the devil was Dayna involved in?

The question ricocheted around in Luke's head as she waved him to a seat with the same lack of enthusiasm she'd shown when she'd offered a drink.

He took one of the overstuffed chairs. She sat across from him on the couch. Her white sweater and gray slacks formed a stark contrast to the colorful flowered cushions. Exercising iron will, Luke ignored the shadowy swell of her breasts displayed by the V-necked sweater and kept his gaze on her face.

"I'm sorry about yanking you out of the B-2 detachment. I know how much your career means to you."

She should, her tone implied. He was the one who'd suggested they put their relationship on hold so he could focus on his flying.

Luke let the dig slide. This wasn't the time to re-hash old hurts. "Yeah, well, I probably didn't help matters by grabbing you on the street yesterday. Or by showing up at the practice round this morning."

"No, you didn't."

He waited while she worked through her way around to the explanation he'd demanded. It was slow in coming.

"I told you Mike and I work special projects for the government."

He tried to imagine what kind of special project would involve a charity golf tournament, an Olympic gold medalist and a military sharpshooter. The possibilities put a kink in his gut.

"What are you? CIA? FBI?"

"Neither. We're employed on an as-needed basis by a small agency, one you've never heard of. Our boss reports directly to the President."

Good God! Was that Dayna sitting there, calmly informing him she operated only one step removed from the President of the United States?

"Okay, here's the deal." Leaning forward, she deposited her ale bottle on the coffee table. "Our government thinks there's a possibility Wu Kim Li and her father may want to defect."

"Tigress Wu?"

Luke gave a low whistle. Like everyone else in the universe, he'd been bombarded by visual images of the teenage megastar since she'd first exploded onto the international sports scene. North Korea touted her as their biggest export since white rice. Luke could only guess at the millions she brought her country in terms of PR *and* cold, hard cash. They'd lose more than face if the girl jumped ship.

"Mike and I are here to determine if the possibility has basis in fact," Dayna said crisply. "If so, we'll make it happen."

"Just like that? The two of you will simply whisk the Wus away from their entourage?"

"We'll have backup available if and when we need it."

Luke was struck by the difference between this contained, self-assured woman and the girl he'd known. His Dayna had held nothing back. She'd been all heart, as passionate when running the river or swinging a club as when she tumbled into bed with him. This Dayna both baffled and intrigued him.

So did her "special project." Frowning, Luke mulled over what she'd told him.

"Something doesn't compute here."

She stiffened. "You think I'm blowing smoke at you?"

"Or not telling me the whole story."

Luke's bottle joined hers on the coffee table. Pinning her with an intent stare, he reasoned out his doubts.

"Wu Kim Li is North Korea's darling. She's as big there as any rock star or movie idol is in the U.S. Giving her and her father asylum in the States would put a serious dent in North Korea's ego, not to mention their relations with the United States."

"Relations between North Korea and the U.S. can hardly get much worse."

"My point exactly. With all the saber-rattling going on over Pyongyang's stated determination to develop nuclear weapons, I can't see our government wanting to make matters worse by stealing away their sweetheart. There's got to be more. What aren't you telling me, Pud?"

The nickname just slipped out, and the fact that Dayna didn't jump down his throat feetfirst told Luke he'd struck a nerve.

Lips pursed, she hesitated for long moments. Weighing her words. Judging his trustworthiness. Luke was about to remind her the United States government trusted him enough to put him at the controls of a super-secret, two-billion-dollar aircraft when she finally unbent.

"Kim Li's father is one of North Korea's foremost nuclear engineers."

"Whoa! I didn't know that."

"Few people do. His government keeps him and his work under pretty tight wraps."

"And now he wants to defect?"

"That's what Mike and I are here to determine."

Well, damn! This was right out of James Bond. A top nuclear scientist seeking asylum. His glamorous daughter going over the wall with him. Dayna smack in the middle of it, orchestrating the whole show.

No wonder she'd been so pissed when Luke had laid that kiss on her and initiated the media clamor over their past affair. She had enough to worry about without having to field questions about an old boyfriend.

"I'm sorry I put you in a box with all this unwelcome publicity," he said gruffly. "Any thoughts about how best to get out of it?"

Blowing out a frustrated breath, she raked a hand through her hair. Luke slammed back the memory of all the times he'd feathered his hands through that silky, sun-streaked mane.

"I think the best option is to play it the way I did at the news conference this morning," she said after a moment. "We have a history. We bumped into each other on the street by mere chance. We got carried away by the moment. We rehashed old times. We went our separate ways. End of story."

"Except we both know it won't end there. Or have you forgotten our Dumpster-diving friend?"

Her face twisted in disgust. "Not hardly."

The incident would have been laughable if it wasn't so outrageous. The controversy had started when some lame, talking head of a commentator expounded on the subject of sexual abstinence as practiced by ancient Olympians. His commentary spawned a fierce media debate as to whether sex relieved stress or diminished the strength of athletes.

The questions put to the modern-day Olympians got so personal and embarrassing that many, including Dayna, refused to respond. Her tight-lipped silence only fueled the speculative fire. Determined to find out how often the Golden Girl had sex with her boyfriend, one of the tabloids had hired some sleazoid to dig through Luke's trash in search of used condoms.

A neighbor had spotted him climbing into the Dumpster and alerted the cops. The resulting publicity had infuriated Dayna and rattled her coach so much that he'd phoned Luke and laid it on the line. He and Dayna had to cool it for a while, let the hype die down, or she could kiss off any hopes of bringing home gold.

History, it seemed, was repeating itself. Same players, different stakes. Except, this time, Luke vowed, he and Dayna would do the manipulating.

"I think we should give them what they want."

"Come again?"

"The media wants a show. We give 'em one."

"I am *not* playing kissy face with you in public, Harper."

"Think about it. You want to deflect attention from your business with Wu Kim Li and her father. I don't want reporters digging too deeply into my presence in the U.K. So we revise our story. Bend the truth to work for both of us."

"No."

"We have to feed them something. It might as well be what we want them to have."

"No."

Exasperated, he folded his arms. "Okay, let's hear some alternatives."

"I can think of several. The first involves you ejecting from your cockpit without a parachute."

"What's number two?"

"You ejecting through the canopy without a helmet."

His lips twitched. "Is there a number three?"

No, dammit, there wasn't. Not one that didn't require death or dismemberment, anyway. Dayna fumed for several moments before admitting as much.

"So where does that leave us?" Luke asked.

"Playing kissy face in public," she conceded, sulking.

They spent the next twenty minutes hammering out a believable blend of fact and fiction:

Sports Illustrated had run an article last month about Dayna's work at the outdoor sports clinic. True.

Luke had read the article and e-mailed her. False.

She'd entered the Pro-Am Charity Tournament at the last minute, thinking they might hook up while she was in Scotland. Also false.

They'd bumped into each other unexpectedly on the street outside her hotel. True.

The meeting had released emotions they'd thought long dead. True again, except the emotions so released were anything but loverlike.

Now Luke was on leave, taking ten days away from his military so he could watch Dayna compete in the tournament. A quick call to his boss would make that true.

"With a little luck and a lot of grandstanding," he said when they finished firming up the details, "that should keep attention focused on us instead of what type aircraft I fly or your side conversations with Wu Kim Li."

It was the grandstanding that worried Dayna.

"Just don't get carried away," she warned. "We'll tell them we learned from our past mistakes. Insist we're taking it slowly this time, not rushing in as fast or as recklessly as we did before."

"Right."

He leaned back in his chair, surveying her from beneath his lashes. His hazel eyes conveyed both speculation and anticipation.

"When do you want to kick off the campaign?"

"This is as good a time as any," she conceded. "I'm doing an autographing at Cockburren's Golf and Antiquities Shop. Kim Li will be there, too, so we can count on some press. You might as well accompany me."

"You'll have to display a little more enthusiasm for my company if you want to make this believable."

"Don't push your luck, Harper."

"Luke," he countered sardonically. "C'mon, Dayna. You can say it."

"Don't push me," she warned again. "Wait here. I need to brief Mike on the new game plan."

He used the brief interval to decompress. Sitting across from Dayna, watching her shoulders hunch when she leaned forward to make a point, doing his damndest to keep his glance away from the shadowy V of her sweater, had just about wrung him dry.

"Mike thinks putting up a smokescreen is a good idea," she informed him curtly when she returned.

"You want to call your boss and arrange for leave while I change?"

She'd have to display *considerably* more enthusiasm for his company, Luke thought wryly as he pulled out his cell phone.

With the wind still raking in off the sea, Dayna exchanged her thin cotton sweater for a pink cashmere turtleneck and a Pendleton wool jacket in soft heather tweed. Her fanny pack rested comfortably on her hip as she and Luke walked to Cockburren's.

It was a short walk. St. Andrews was a small university town with a population that normally hovered around eighteen thousand. Major tournaments like the British Open or the Women's International Pro-Am Charity swelled that number greatly but took nothing away from the charm of the ancient town.

The granite buildings lining its streets had been aged by the centuries into a patchwork of gray and black. Every second or third shop window, it seemed, displayed equipment, art or clothing for the sport the Scots claimed as their own. Sandwiched in between the shops were lively restaurants and pubs.

The ghostly spires of St. Andrews' once-magnificent abbey thrust into the sky at the upper end of Market Street. On the lower end of the street, the towers and turrets of the university dominated the view. Dayna and Luke threaded their way along the walkway, bumping elbows with tourists and students sporting heavy backpacks slung over their shoulders and iPod cords snaking from jacket pockets.

Luke put a hand to the small of her back to steer her past a boisterous group of students. "I don't know how much you know about the university," he commented.

She was wearing several layers of wool and cashmere, for Pete's sake! There was no reason on earth she should feel more than the slight pressure of his hand. Disgusted by the shivers that danced down her spine, Dayna disguised her reaction to his touch with a shrug.

"Only that it's one of the oldest in Scotland."

"*The* oldest in Scotland. Best I recall, it was founded somewhere around 1400."

Why did he leave his palm resting just above the swell of her rear? Was he already slipping into his role in their agreed-upon act?

"John Witherspoon, one of the signers of our Declaration of Independence, graduated from here. So did William Arthur Philip Louis Mountbatten-Windsor."

"Prince William?" she guessed.

"The one and only. I never ran into him myself, but Alan Parks stood him and some of his chums to a round at one of the pubs."

"Sounds like Alan Parks. Judging by our brief

encounter, I'd say your fellow pilot has never met a stranger."

"You pegged him. Here, this is Cockburren's."

Increasing the pressure, he ushered her through the door of a shop wedged between a bakery and a clothier with a colorful display of kilts in the front windows. Several of the LPGA stars were already present, chatting with fans or signing autographs.

A quick glance showed Kim Li sitting at a table in an alcove. A number of her entourage were also present. Dayna recognized her trainer and the thin, intense individual who acted as her manager.

"Miss Duncan!"

Smiling from ear to ear, a distinguished gentleman in a black vest, ruffled shirt and tartan pants maneuvered through the crowd.

"Welcome!" His accent combined a musical blend of English and Scottish brogue. "I'm Archibald Cockburren, owner of the shop. We're so pleased you could join us."

"Thank you for inviting me. This is Luke Harper, an old friend of mine."

"Ah, yes. Wasn't that your picture I saw in the paper this morning, Captain Harper?"

"It was."

"How fortunate that you and Ms. Duncan found each other again."

"We think so."

Hooking his arm around Dayna's waist, Luke drew her against him like a long-lost lover newly reunited with his one and only.

"Hold that pose!"

The command came from one of the reporters clustered around Kim Li. The girl's mouth took a downturn when the reporters abandoned her to swarm the new arrivals, but she didn't remain out of the limelight for long. Sauntering across the shop, Kim Li insinuated herself into the eager circle surrounding Dayna and Luke.

"I, too, see picture in paper." With a kittenish smile, she offered Luke her hand. "Now understand why Dayna play so well today."

"As you did," he responded. "I saw you hole out on number seventeen. Wish I could line up putts like that."

"Dayna no teach you to putt?" Tch-tching, the Korean shook her head. "No matter. I am very good teacher. I give you lesson."

Dayna kept her jaw from dropping. Barely. She'd been trying to establish a connection with Wu Kim Li for two days. Luke had managed it in two minutes—while standing with his arm still looped around Dayna's waist, no less.

She wouldn't put it past the sexy eighteen-year-old to issue an even less subtle invitation. Cringing inside at the prospect of headlines trumpeting a potential love triangle, she nodded to the autograph seekers queued up by the table.

"Looks like we've got lots of folks waiting for us. Shall we get to work?"

Chapter 6

The opportunity Dayna had been hoping for came midway through the autographing session.

A beaming Archibald Cockburren invited everyone in the store to enjoy an afternoon tea supplied by the bakery next door. Lured by trays of cucumber sandwiches, fruit tarts and warm scones begging to be slathered with strawberry jam and frothy cream, the crowd drifted toward the lavish display.

Dayna kept one eye on Kim Li while responding to the eager questions of two kayaking enthusiasts who'd crashed the golf soiree to corner her.

"Have you tried the River Orchay, Ms. Duncan?

With the spring runoff, it grows to a stonking grade five."

Young and brimming with eagerness, the two university students reminded Dayna of herself in her reckless youth.

"I have," she confirmed, "but my favorite run here in Scotland is the River Findhorn gorge."

"Oh, aye! The spring melt in the Monadhliath Mountains makes that a bonny paddle indeed."

"Will you have time to hit the water whilst you're here?" the younger of the two asked hopefully. "There's a foine stretch of white in Perthshire, less than an hour from St. Andrews. Chloe and I would be honored to put our paddles in with yours."

"I might take you up on that if I don't make the cut for the final round of the tournament."

"Och, there's no fear of that happening!"

From the corner of one eye, Dayna spotted her target drifting toward a display of antique golf gear. Kim Li was momentarily alone. She'd left both fans and handlers scarfing down scones and fruit tarts.

At that moment Luke moved into Dayna's line of sight. His broad shoulders blocked her view of Kim Li handlers—and their view of her. Luke's small, almost imperceptible nod told Dayna he'd intended precisely that.

She wasted no time detaching herself from the kay-akers. With a smile and a promise to let them know if she decided to take to the water, she joined Kim Li.

"We didn't get to finish our conversation in the sauna this morning," she said, her voice low.

The girl darted a nervous look behind her. "No, we did not."

"You told your partner at Cypress Point that you would be here in St. Andrews. You stressed that your father would, too."

"How do you know what I tell her?"

"She passed your message along, as we think you intended her to."

With another furtive glance over her shoulder, Kim Li leaned closer. "We?" she whispered. "Who is we?"

Dayna wasn't about to mention the U.S. govern-ment until she got confirmation of Wu's intentions.

"People who want to help you and your father establish residence in the United States…if that's your desire."

"Yes."

The whisper was soft and desperate.

"We can go tonight," Dayna murmured, testing the waters. "I'll arrange for you and your father to…"

"No, no! Cannot go until last day of tournament. After I win, there will be much demand for inter-views, many chances to get away from my watchers."

Dayna refrained from suggesting Wu might not win the tournament.

"You must talk to father," Kim Li whispered. "Must tell him plan."

"My partner will contact your father. He'll identify himself by the code name Hawk. Together, we'll make sure both you and your father know the plan before we put it into operation."

Kim Li angled just enough to take in Luke's broad shoulders, still blocking the view of those in the front of the shop.

"He is your partner?"

"No. He's window dressing." Seeing more explanation was required, Dayna elaborated. "He's a diversion. I'm using him to deflect attention from my business with you."

A speculative gleam lit the girl's eyes. "Your romance not real?"

Oh, Lord! The last thing this op needed was for the target to start sniffing around Luke with the idea of adding him to her trophy case.

"It's real," Dayna lied, sinking further into the quagmire that was Luke Harper.

Kim Li pouted but seemed to accept that. "When we speak again?"

"After the qualifying rounds. I'll try to arrange it so we play together in the finals."

"If you make cut."

Dayna's back teeth ground together. First Lightning, then Mackenzie. Now this obnoxious teen.

"I'll make the cut."

Like the first qualifying round, the second required intense concentration.

There was no wind, thank God, only an early-morning haze that soon burned off. The sun came out midway through the competition, sparkling on the bay and warming the air so much that Dayna removed the jacket of her wind suit.

To her fierce satisfaction, she posted the fourth lowest score of the day. Fans and sportscasters alike swarmed her when she walked off the eighteenth green. After a wave of clamorous congratulations, they gave ground to the man who shouldered his way through the crowd.

In jeans, a blue oxford shirt and his leather bomber jacket, Luke Harper carried himself with the confidence that marked him as an officer and leader of men.

"Great round, Puddles."

It was bad enough that every fuzzy-coated microphone extended over the heads of the crowd picked up his comment. Luke's wicked grin compounded the felony. Dayna could see he wasn't the least bit sorry about broadcasting the ridiculous nickname to the entire world.

"I'll get you for that," she murmured as she tipped her head for their second kiss.

The first had taken her by surprise. Given their decision to play to the cameras, she should have been prepared for this one. *Should* being the operative word. The sparks it ignited were as unexpected as they were disconcerting.

Her mind made instant excuses for her body's eager reaction. She was just jazzed from the terrific round. Still thrumming with the thrill of victory. Her pumped-up endorphins magnified the heat generated by the kiss and fired it into a bright blaze.

Despite the determined rationalization, it took a concentrated effort of will to break the contact and stand in the circle of Luke's arm while she responded to the flurry of questions. One query came zinging her way above the heads of the crowd.

"What do you and Captain Harper have planned during the break between rounds?"

Tournament officials had crammed the so-called "break" with events that ranged from a traditional bagpipe skirl to a children's golf clinic. Dayna had donated an hour at the clinic. The rest of the day she intended to spend finalizing the details of the plan to extract the Wus. Luke wasn't included in either of these activities, but Dayna could hardly admit as much publicly.

"We're just taking it easy," she said with deliberate vagueness.

"Together?" the persistent reporter wanted to know.

Dayna merely smiled, waved to the crowd and walked up the slope to the clubhouse with Luke at her side. They parted company at the entrance.

"I'll meet you back at the hotel."

"Sure you want to?" she asked. "I'm considering several forms of severe retribution in retaliation for you feeding that nickname to the press."

"Forewarned is forearmed." Unrepentant, he tugged on her ponytail and dropped another kiss on her nose. "I'll wear my flak vest."

The cameras, Dayna reminded herself sternly as she made her way to the officiating table to turn in her scorecard. He was playing to the cameras.

Yet damned if she didn't take the tingle with her into the locker room. She'd come off the course too late to catch Kim Li in the sauna. The girl was already stretched out on the portable massage table, being pummeled by sumo-mama.

The masseuse kneaded Kim Li's bare back, but her unblinking stare followed Dayna as she nodded to Kim Li and went to the storage facility to stow her gear.

* * *

The residue of that stare stayed with Dayna during the short walk back to the hotel.

Did the masseuse suspect something? Had one of her cohorts observed the brief colloquy between Dayna and Kim Li at Cockburren's? Was Hawk receiving the same vibes from Dr. Wu's guard dogs? Anxious to connect with her partner and get his take on these sudden, prickly doubts, Dayna keyed the lock to her hotel room.

Her mind might have been on the Wus but her instincts responded instantly to the shape that materialized when she opened the door. It came at her from off to the right, unexpected and unexplained.

Dayna swung around. Luke's face and form registered just in time to halt the knee she had halfway to his groin.

"Whoa!" Hastily, he backed out of range. "You weren't kidding about retribution."

"I wasn't trying to exact retribution, you idiot. Not yet, anyway." Disgusted, she slammed the door. "A swift knee to the gonads is my normal response to men who pop out from behind doors unexpectly."

"I'll remember that."

"How did you get into my room?"

"The maid saw us on TV." His mouth tipped. "We must be giving a convincing performance."

She couldn't argue with that. An all-too-vivid reminder of their kiss hit her as she unclipped her fanny pack and tossed it on the sofa. Only then did she notice the champagne bucket and crystal flute poised on a heavy silver tray.

"What's this?"

"Room service delivered it, compliments of the house for your terrific round. Why don't I get a glass from the bar and we'll celebrate together?"

"I don't have time to celebrate. I need to talk to Hawk and…"

"Hawk?"

"Mike Callahan. His code name—call sign, as you flyboys term it—is Hawkeye."

"I'll bet his call sign has something to do with the marksmanship patch on his pocket."

"You'd win the bet."

Showing no signs of leaving, Luke followed her into the sitting room. "What's your call sign?"

"Rogue. After the Rogue River in Oregon," she added when he lifted an inquiring brow. "That's where I first learned to paddle. *Not* in a puddle, as you insist on insinuating with that ridiculous nickname."

"Think of the nickname as another diversion. Wouldn't you rather have the media focusing on it and our off-course activities than speculating on your sudden friendship with Wu Kim Li?"

The media wasn't all she had to worry about. Still feeling the needle of sumo-mama's intense scrutiny, Dayna massaged the back of her neck. Luke watched her for a moment, then crossed to the ice bucket.

"You played a heck of a game, Duncan. You need to celebrate. More to the point, you need to relax."

The hotel's very efficient room service—or a very confident Luke—had already popped the champagne cork. An elaborate silver stopper in the shape of a thistle preserved the wine's bubbles.

Removing the stopper, Luke poured a stream of pale gold into the crystal flute. "Here. Sit down, drink this and let me work out some of the kinks."

What the hell, Dayna thought. If a massage worked for Kim Li, it could work for her. She could certainly use some unkinking.

Accepting the champagne, she sank onto the sofa and unzipped her windbreaker. The cushions dipped as Luke sat behind her and tucked her ponytail out of the way. When he went to work on her stiff muscles, she groaned.

"Oh, God! You're good."

"That's what they all say," he returned with a smile in his voice. "So are you, by the way. I still don't believe the putt you sank on number seven."

His breath was a warm wash against her cheek. His hands worked sheer magic.

"Neither do I," she murmured.

"And your drive on number twelve. That was majesty in motion."

Sabotaged by the compliment and his clever, clever hands, Dayna had to agree. That drive *had* been pretty spectacular.

"Thanks."

She tipped the champagne to her lips. The fizz teased her nostrils and added to the seduction of his touch.

"It felt like old times," he commented. "Watching you compete, whooping and cheering with the rest of the crowd."

His hands stilled for a moment.

"I hated that I missed the Olympics, Dayna. You don't know how much I wanted to see you win gold."

The old hurts put out their spiky tentacles, piercing her pleasure. She'd wanted him there, too. So badly that standing on the winner's platform, listening to the national anthem, watching the Stars and Stripes being hoisted, had filled her with as much regret as joy.

She'd never admitted that to anyone. Her coach. Her parents. Her friends. Even Gillian Ridgeway, who'd become as close as a sister these past months. Burying her nose in the crystal flute, Dayna tried to drown the lingering resentment. It wouldn't die.

"You could have been there," she heard herself say.

"I know."

"You were the one who decided we should cool it. Not me."

"I know."

Maybe it was the champagne. Or the itchy awareness of his chest only inches from her back. Or the slow, kneading rhythm when he resumed the massage.

Or all of the above, Dayna thought on another wave of resentment. This one was so swift and strong it almost made her feel woozy.

"Why *weren't* you there, Harper?" Riding the wave, she twisted around to face him. "Why didn't you think we were worth fighting for?"

He didn't dodge the question or the raw emotions it evoked. "I knew what the Olympics meant to you. Hell, the last weekend we spent together your palms were so blistered from paddling you had to slather on antiseptic ointment and wear cotton gloves the whole time. You think I wanted to get in the way of that kind of drive, that kind of dedication?"

Dayna's lip curled. Every moment of their last weekend was so vivid in her mind she might have been back at Columbus Air Force Base instead of in this cozy suite filled with chintz-covered furniture and dark oak trim. Her heart racing, she debunked his quiet explanation.

"Don't give me that noble sacrifice crap. You explained everything in precise detail. You'd just entered the most intensive phase of pilot training. You were in class or flying all day, studying every night. You didn't have the time or the inclination for a long-distance love affair. Not that there was much love involved in our affair," she added. "Lust, maybe, but not love."

"Lust, definitely." Stung but obviously trying to hang on to his temper, he grinned. "That hasn't changed, has it? Or did I misread the signals when we locked lips a while ago?"

Dayna shoved off the sofa, so incensed by the grin that her heart pounded like a jackhammer and black spots danced in front of her eyes.

"Damn straight you misread the signals! Do you think I enjoy performing with you in front of the cameras like a trained seal?"

"Matter of fact, I do." Jaw locked, he rose, as well. "You didn't exactly push me away this afternoon, Pud."

"Do...not...call...me...that!"

Anger held her in such a tight vise she couldn't seem to breathe. This was insane! Where had all this roiling emotion come from? She'd put Luke Harper out of her life years ago. Out of her head. This crazy situation had thrown them together again, sure, but...but...

But what?

She fisted a hand, shoved it against her breastbone. Why couldn't she think? Why couldn't she breathe?

"Dayna?"

She staggered toward him. One step. That's all she took, all she could manage. Luke leaped forward and caught her as she started to crumple.

"Dayna, what's wrong!"

She sagged against him, unable to speak, unable to breathe. Her heart felt as though it was about to explode. Panting, she fought for air.

"I… I…"

She clutched her chest, felt the room spin. Her vision blurred, darkening around the edges, until all she could see was Luke's face.

"Hang on, sweetheart. Hang on." Mouth tight, eyes grim, he eased her to the carpeted floor. "I'm calling a doctor."

She dug her nails into his forearms.

"And…Hawk."

Chapter 7

With Dayna curled in a tight fetal position on the floor, Luke lunged across the room. He snatched up the phone and stabbed 0 for the hotel operator. In the two-second lifetime it took for the operator to come on, he ransacked his memory bank for the emergency medical procedures drilled into him during his USAF Survival, Evasion, Resistance and Escape training.

SERE had focused on basic, rough-and-ready medicine to treat injuries suffered by downed aircrews after bailing out or crashing behind enemy lines. Luke had learned to counter shock, improvise splints and shoot lifesaving medications directly into veins and arteries.

He'd also learned to recognize the signs of apparent heart attack. His own chest cramping at the sight of Dayna's white, pasty face contorted in pain, Luke dragged the phone across the room with him.

"We need an ambulance!" he bit out when the operator came on. "Room 224."

He was on his knees, rolling Dayna onto her back, before the startled operator stammered a response.

"Yes, s-sir! Room 224."

"Send up an AED if there's one in the hotel."

"Send what?"

What did the friggin' initials stand for? Luke had no clue.

"One of those portable defibrillators."

"Yes, sir. Please, stay on the line while I…"

The receiver hit the floor. He'd keep the line open, but he knew every second counted. He had to assess Dayna's condition and *fast.*

She was conscious, thank God! And breathing, but every erratic rise and fall of her chest brought a grunt of pain.

Clamping an iron lid over the fear that ripped through him at those agonized breaths, Luke pressed two fingers to the side of her neck. Her pulse beat against his hand with the ferocity of a jungle drum. At least she hadn't gone into cardiac arrest. Not yet, anyway.

"Dayna. Sweetheart. An ambulance is on the way. Has this happened before? Are you taking medication for a heart condition?"

"N-no."

"How about aspirin? Do you have any in the bathroom?"

"No."

"Okay, just lie still. I'm going to elevate your feet."

She gripped his arm before he could drag the cushions from the sofa. "Call…Hawk."

Hell, he'd forgotten about Callahan! The man was Dayna's partner. Maybe she had a medical condition he knew how to treat. Yanking his cell phone from his shirt pocket, Luke flipped up the lid.

"We need to keep the hotel line open. I'll have to dial the hotel to get…"

"Use…my watch."

Panting, she lifted her wrist. Her shaking fingers fumbled over the face of an expensive-looking chronometer, but a sudden spasm had her clawing at her chest again.

His heart in his throat, Luke grasped her wrist. "How do I do this?"

"Push…top left…knob." Sweat beaded on her forehead. "Three…times."

He jabbed his thumb over the knob and once again reached for the cushions. Mere seconds later Callahan's terse reply cut through Dayna's rasping breaths.

"Acknowledging emergency signal. Advise of situation."

A distant corner of Luke's mind noted the incredible clarity of the transmission. Whatever was packed into that thin watch beat even the B-2's ultra-sophisticated Milstar communications system.

"Do I have to push another knob to respond? Pud! How do I respond?"

"I hear you, Harper," Callahan shot back. "What's happening?"

"Dayna's in severe distress, pulse elevated and highly erratic, breathing labored. I've called for an ambulance. Does she have a medical condition the EMTs need to know about?"

"Negative. Where are you?"

"Her hotel room."

"I'm on my way. ETA ten to twelve minutes."

After that there was nothing to do but try to keep her comfortable. Settling onto the floor beside her, Luke pillowed her head in his lap. His tone remained calm, his hand steady as he brushed her hair back from her sweat-streaked forehead, but his insides twisted with every gasp.

"Lie still, Puddles. I'm right here with you. Just lie still.

He wasn't sure when she started to breathe easier. Some moments after the hotel operator's tremulous voice came through the receiver, advising that the ambulance should arrive within minutes.

"I've notified Mr. Woodhouse, our director of security," the operator added. "He's on his way up."

"Thanks."

Was Dayna's color coming back? Afraid he was seeing what he wanted to see, Luke brushed a knuckle over her cheek.

"Did you hear that? The cavalry's on the way."

"I…heard."

The awful rasping gave way to slower, less agonized breaths. Luke curved his hand over her throat to check her pulse. It was still dancing to a jungle beat but not as wildly as before.

"Your pulse is slowing, Pud."

Her lids lifted. Through the screen of her lashes, she telegraphed a reluctant surrender. "Can't seem… to break you of…that."

"What?" With his fear for her overriding everything else, he hadn't realized he'd let the hated nickname slip out. "Oh, you mean, Puddles?"

"Guess I'll have to…get used to it."

Luke managed to keep from shouting his relief.

She was most definitely doing better. Grinning, he stroked her cheek again.

"Guess so."

She dragged in another breath. Deeper. Steadier.

He did the same, pulling in the first full measure of air since Dayna had clutched her chest.

"I think I can sit up now," she said, her breathing almost back to normal.

"No need to push it."

"I'm okay now, Luke. Really." She put a hand to her sternum and knuckled the valley between her breasts. "The pain is gone."

"That doesn't mean you're okay."

They both jumped when the door rattled under a fierce pounding.

"Ms. Duncan! This is hotel security."

"She's here," Luke shouted. "Come in."

Using his master key card, the hotel's director of security rushed into the suite. Squat, broad-shouldered and bull-necked, he brought two minions in with him. One carried a portable defibrillator in a white plastic case with a red heart on the cover. All three looked relieved when they found Dayna sitting up instead of stretched out on the floor.

"Is your chest hurting, Ms. Duncan?"

"Not as much as it was."

"Rest easy, then. A National Health Service Ambulance is on the way."

Too shaken by those terrifying moments when her heart had almost galloped out of her chest to argue, Dayna slumped against Luke's solid bulk. His arms came around her, as warm and comforting as his voice had been mere minutes ago.

She was still in their protective circle when the thud of footsteps announced the arrival of the EMT squad. Wheeling in a stretcher, they snapped on plastic gloves and crouched beside Dayna.

"Are you feeling pain, Ms. Duncan?"

"Not now."

"When you did, how would you describe it?"

"Like my heart was in the lead at Ascot."

Hawk pounded into the room at that moment. His glance cut instantly to Dayna.

"You okay?"

"Yes."

"What happened?"

Luke pushed to his feet. "I'll fill you in while the EMTs do their work. Let's get out of their way."

Feeling disconcertingly bereft without his comforting warmth, Dayna shoved up her sleeve and held out her arm. One EMT tech attached a blood pressure cuff. The other threaded out the leads for a portable EKG machine.

When she was hooked to the monitor, the tech transmitted the results by cell phone to the E.R. At the same time he examined the narrow strip spewing out of the machine. After studying the steady pattern, he consulted with his partner before pronouncing Dayna alive and still kicking.

"Your vitals and EKG appear to be normal, Ms. Duncan, but we need to transport you to hospital for more tests."

She could envision the media frenzy that would erupt if they wheeled her through the hotel lobby on a stretcher.

"We don't need to tie up an ambulance. I'll drive to the hospital."

"The hell you will!"

"No way!"

The simultaneous protests burst from Luke and Hawk. Dayna corrected herself with a grimace.

"One of these gentlemen will drive me."

The EMT techs looked doubtful.

"I'm fine now," she insisted. "Really."

She underscored the point by folding her legs under her and gliding to her feet before any of the men present could reach out to help her. When the EMTs packed up their gear, she supplied the necessary information for insurance purposes.

"Thank you so much for your quick response." Her

grateful smile included the hotel's security director and his minions. "Can I show my appreciation by arranging VIP passes for you to the tournament?"

"You're not thinking of finishing the tournament?" the hotel's security director asked with a frown.

"Depends on what the docs at the hospital say."

Hawk and Luke weren't as easy to palm off. When the others had departed, Dayna confronted two males wearing almost identical scowls.

"Forget the tournament," Luke ordered. His hand wrapped around her upper arm. "You're going to the hospital."

"Yes, I am, but…"

"No buts," Hawk said flatly. Scooping up her fanny pack, he took her other arm. "Let's go."

Feeling like a prisoner shackled between two burly guards, Dayna was marched toward the door. Halfway there, she dug in her heels.

"Wait!"

Her gaze locked on the champagne bottle tipped at an angle in the silver bucket. Something tugged at the edge of her mind. Something about the bottle, or the cork, or…

A sudden image razored into her head. Like a digital movie played on a high-definition screen, she saw Luke removing the elaborate silver stopper and pouring a pale gold stream into a crystal flute.

One crystal flute.

An ugly suspicion formed, and was instantly swept away. He'd offered to get another glass from the bathroom and would have joined her in a drink. Yet Dayna couldn't shake the nagging sense that she was missing something.

"Didn't you say room service delivered that?"

"What?"

"The champagne." Pulling free of her shackles, she turned to face him. "Room service delivered it?"

"They did."

"Did you pop the cork?"

"No." He paused, and a grim understanding dawned in his eyes. "The bottle was wearing that thistle stopper when the waiter carried in the bucket and tray."

She was probably way out in left field. She had absolutely no reason to suspect someone had tampered with the champagne—aside from the fact that she knew she was in top physical condition and had never experienced any heart problems before.

Going on pure instinct, she turned to Hawk. He'd remained silent during the exchange, but his tight expression told her he hadn't missed its significance.

"I think Luke better drive me to the hospital while you contact our friends in British Intelligence. Tell them we need a lab analysis ASAP."

"Roger that. I'll also brief Lightning. Call me from the hospital when you know something."

Dayna's energy and strength had returned full force by the time she finished the battery of tests ordered by the E.R. doc. Luke stepped outside the exam room for some of the more intimate tests, but muscled his way back in to hear the results.

"Everything appears normal," the Pakistani-born E.R. doc confirmed. "Despite the lack of indicators, however, we can't rule out possible heart problems."

Her dark eyes reflected utter seriousness as she regarded the patient perched on the edge of the exam table.

"Something caused your bout of severe arrhythmia, Ms. Duncan. Stress, the physical demands of your job, your exertion on the links this afternoon— all these factors added together would put tremendous strain on anyone."

Not to mention the small matter of whisking a nuclear scientist and his daughter away from their watchdogs.

"I've also seen reports on the telly of your reunion with Captain Harper," the doc continued. Her serious mien gave way to a smile that included Luke. "It's so very romantic, the two of you finding each other again. I was quite swept away by it all. I can see how you would be, as well."

Dayna swallowed a groan and ignored the wicked glint that sprang into Luke's eyes.

"You said you were with Captain Harper when you suffered this attack," the physician continued. "You also mentioned that he was… How did you phrase it? Helping to work out the kinks from your game."

Dayna couldn't remember the last time she'd blushed, but the gentle insinuation sent heat rushing into her cheeks.

"Captain Harper was massaging my neck. We weren't having sex."

"No?" Her mouth twitching, the doc slanted Luke a sideways glance. "How unfortunate."

Oh, brother! First Kim Li. Now this slender, doe-eyed physician. Luke was reeling 'em in. Pointedly, Dayna cleared her throat.

"Are we done here?"

"We are."

All brisk business now, the doctor handed over a stack of appointment slips.

"I've scheduled you for an echocardiogram, a nuclear treadmill test and a follow-up appointment with our on-staff cardiologist."

The appointments, Dayna saw, were spread over the next three days. "I might have to adjust the times. I don't know my schedule for the rest of the tournament."

"I'm sorry, Ms. Duncan, but it's highly unlikely you'll be able to finish the tournament. I'm required to file a report on any E.R. visits by foreign nationals with the National Health Service, you see. NHS will notify tournament officials. If they permitted you to proceed without medical clearance, they would be held liable should you suffer another attack while on the course."

Dayna had participated in too many big-dollar sports events to suggest that she sign a release freeing the organizers from liability. Such agreements weren't worth the paper they were written on if and when lawyers got involved.

The whole issue could be moot, she reminded herself, depending on the lab analysis of the champagne. Until then, she had no choice but to complete the additional tests. Luckily, tomorrow was a down day. She'd use the break to whip through this battery of tests.

"All I have on the agenda tomorrow are PR appearances. Any chance we can reschedule these appointments and get the results in time for me to play on Friday?"

"I'll see what I can do."

The physician returned a few moments later with

a revised schedule. "We can do the echocardiogram this afternoon, but the nuclear treadmill test requires several hours and can't be done until tomorrow morning. You must report to radiology at nine."

"She will," Luke promised.

The doc turned to him with another melting smile. "I would also advise that she get some rest."

"She will."

"You know," Dayna said heavily when the physician had departed, "I *can* speak for myself."

"I know. Let's go get this echocardiogram out of the way."

"You don't have to stay for that. I'm feeling fine now, Luke. Really."

The look he gave her would have stripped the rust from a junkyard car. Silenced, she walked with him through a maze of corridors and down a narrow flight of stairs to the radiology department.

The sonogram of her heart took less than half an hour. Dayna emerged from the subterranean darkness into what was left of the afternoon. She was still wearing her cobalt-colored Gore-Tex jacket and pants, but clouds obscured the sun and the air had a bite to it.

"Here, put this on." Shrugging out of his leather jacket, Luke draped it over her shoulders. "The wind's picked up again."

She didn't see how it could blow any stronger without setting off sirens. With a pang of sympathy for any unfortunate foursomes still out on the course, she slid her arms into the jacket. The scent of leather and Luke teased at her as he took her elbow. Once ensconced in the privacy of his car, she fingered her chronometer.

"I need to let Hawk know what the doc said."

"Go ahead."

While Luke steered through the cobbled streets of St. Andrews, Dayna delivered a succinct report. She brought Hawk up to speed and was about to ask if he'd contacted Lightning when a street sign caught her eye.

"Hang on a sec, Hawk." Slewing around, she checked the sign again. "You missed the turn," she told Luke.

"No, I didn't."

"The hotel is behind us."

"We're not going back to the hotel."

"Where *are* we going?"

"A hunting lodge just north of Dundee."

"Who decided that?"

"I did, when the doc said you needed rest. You won't get it at the hotel when word of your trip to the E.R. leaks, which you know it will. The phone will ring off the hook. And if they can't reach you by phone, they'll set up camp outside your hotel room."

Hawk had heard the brief exchange and agreed with Luke. "I'll take care of things at this end. You're off the op until we know what caused that kick to your heart."

"'Scuse me. Last time I checked, there was the small matter of two targets to work. You can't handle both."

"I was just waiting to hear from you before I contact Lightning. He can send in another operative if necessary."

Dayna's mouth thinned to a tight line. This was her op, dammit. She'd studied every facet of Wu Kim Li's personality and game before jumping a plane for Scotland. Once here, she'd worked to establish contact with the girl and lay the groundwork for the snatch.

Those terrifying moments at the hotel when she couldn't get her breath were already almost forgotten. *Almost.* Just enough residual memory remained for Dayna to concede she'd be more of a liability than an asset to Hawk if she suffered another attack like that.

Then there was Luke. Judging by the stubborn set to his jaw, she'd have to put her gun to his head to get him to turn the car around. Even then he'd probably insist she pull the trigger before he'd comply.

Thoroughly disgruntled at having the ground yanked out from under her, Dayna yielded with something less than graciousness.

"Okay, okay. I'll take the treadmill test in the

morning and we'll go from there. In the meantime, you work that lab analysis on the champagne."

"The bottle is on its way to the forensics lab in Edinburgh as we speak."

"Call me as soon as you hear from them."

"Will do. Now, why don't you just sit back, relax and enjoy the scenery."

"Yeah, right."

Chapter 8

Lightning was reviewing the previous night's activity summary from agents in the field when Gillian came in with word she had Hawkeye on the secure line.

"He needs to talk to you," Jilly reported with a worried crease between her brows. "I think something's happened to Rogue."

Knowing how close she and Dayna had become, Nick didn't object when she lingered in his office but took the precaution of *not* putting Hawk on speaker. OMEGA rarely lost an operative. When they did, the details weren't pretty.

"Lightning here. What's happening, Hawk?"

"Rogue suffered a severe bout of chest pains and had to go to the E.R."

Nick's knuckles went white where he gripped the phone. He'd braced himself for guns, knives, a vicious wire garrote cutting into the throat. Not this. Not Rogue. She kept herself in such superb condition she could run rings around any other OMEGA operative, her boss included.

"Is she okay?"

"She thinks she is. She refused to ride to the hospital in an ambulance. Insisted she'd drive herself until we nixed that."

"We?"

"Luke Harper was with her when she had the attack."

"Thank God someone was. Was it a heart attack?"

"Rogue?" Jilly gasped. "Is he talking about Rogue?"

Nodding, Nick keyed the speaker button. If Rogue required immediate extraction and transport home, Jilly would arrange it. She needed to hear the details.

"I'm putting you on speaker, Hawk. Jilly's here with me. Was it a heart attack?" he asked again.

"The docs termed it severe arrhythmia, possibly brought on by stress or physical overexertion. Rogue's not so sure."

Jilly's eyes rounded as Hawk related Dayna's suspicions about the champagne she'd been sipping right before her attack.

"The Brits promised a lab analysis ASAP. In the meantime, the docs think Rogue should undergo a thorough cardiac evaluation."

"Does she want it done there, or should we bring her home?"

"Here, although she's not convinced her heart is the problem."

"Whatever caused that arrhythmia," Nick said sharply, "the strain could have damaged her heart muscle. Tell her she's on ice until she completes those tests. And for God's sake, make sure she rests up."

"Harper's taking care of that," Hawk drawled.

"Seems like his name is popping up with some frequency all of a sudden."

"You'll hear it a lot more. He's got Rogue on a short leash right now and sounds like he means to keep her there."

"*Our* Rogue?"

"The one and the same."

Nick tried to imagine anyone curtailing Dayna's activities against her will and failed dismally.

"I need to hear more about that in a minute. First give me an update on the Wus."

"No change from the report I sent earlier. Rogue

confirmed Kim Li wants to defect. Her father has yet to give me a definitive answer. I had planned to work him during the down day tomorrow, but may need to shift my focus to keep a tab on the girl."

"You want me to send in another operative?"

"Depends on whether Rogue's still on ice during the last few days of the tournament. She doesn't want to pull out of it, but unless she gets a green light from the docs she may have no choice."

Jilly hopped off the corner of Nick's desk, her eyes alive with excitement. "I'll take her slot."

For a moment she looked so much like her mother that Nick blinked. He'd been half in love with Maggie Sinclair from their first meeting in Cannes so many years ago. Adam Ridgeway had eventually claimed Maggie and Mackenzie had later turned Nick's life upside down. Yet all he had to do was look at the beautiful, vibrant young woman who was his goddaughter to remember the jolt.

Jilly was going to rock some man's world, he thought ruefully. He just hoped it wasn't the world of the too smooth, too slick Ivy-leaguer who kept trying to put a ring on her finger.

"It's a charity tournament," Jilly said in a rush of eagerness. "The entry fee covers both the initial and final rounds, presuming golfers post a qualifying score. I'll have to check the fine print, but I'll bet there are contingencies to cover withdrawal and/or substitution for medical reasons."

"No!"

The flat refusal erupted from the speaker.

"I'm not as good as Dayna," Jilly continued in a rush, "but I do know which end of a golf club to swing. What's your handicap, Hawk?"

"Golf is only a small part of this op," he countered. "The rest of it could become real dangerous, real fast."

"Which only reinforces the fact that you need someone to watch your back."

"Someone who knows *how* to watch my back. You're not a trained agent. You don't know how to handle yourself in the field."

Lightning was relegated to the sidelines as Jilly planted her palms on his desk and traded verbal punches with one of his toughest agents. Her blue eyes flashing, she gave as good as she got.

"I know enough to feel comfortable walking DC streets at night. Or are you forgetting who taught me how to shoot everything from a single-barrel derringer to a double-ought-thirty?"

"Dammit, Gillian…"

"I also spent almost two years in Beijing. I don't pretend to fully comprehend the Asian mind with all its subtle complexities. But I'll bet I can relate to Wu Kim Li and her father on levels you can't."

"I'll give you that," he conceded, sounding as goaded as a gored bull, "but that's all I'm going to give."

"Is that right? How about the fact that I'm my parents' daughter? If I inherited one-tenth of their combined smarts, I can at least maintain contact with Kim Li while you work her father."

He responded with something close to a growl, and Lightning decided it was time to intervene.

"Get me the details on the tournament, will you, Jilly? I need to talk to Hawk."

The polite request housed an unmistakable command. To her credit, she didn't presume on their close relationship by arguing her case further. She did, however, make a face as she straightened and popped him a salute.

"Yes, sir!"

Nick waited until she'd closed the door to pick up the thread. "Jilly made some excellent points. I'd have to clear it with Maggie and Adam before I allow her to go into the field, but…"

"Yeah, good luck with that!"

"…but this is your op. Yours and Rogue's. The final decision is up to the two of you. Get her take on it and get back to me."

Dayna took the call from Hawk while circling the shore of a small loch ringed by rolling hills. Black-faced sheep grazed the slopes, lifting their heads to peer over stone walls while Luke navigated the narrow road.

Dayna stared back at them in disgust as Hawk confirmed that she was on ice until she got a green light from the docs. The news that Jilly had volunteered to step in spawned mixed emotions. Dayna's initial reaction mirrored Hawk's. The more he argued against the idea, however, the more she saw its potential. If nothing else, Jilly could maintain the tenuous connection with Kim Li until Dayna returned to the scene.

"Sorry, Hawk. I know you don't like the idea, but I think Jilly would make an excellent substitute if I have to pull out of the tournament. She plays a good game, so she'll hold her own on the course, and she's smart."

"Smart people can end up dead in this business."

"She knows that. So does Lightning."

"She doesn't have any field experience."

"Maybe not, but I'm betting she's picked up more operational awareness than any of us realize while filling in for Elizabeth these past weeks."

She was also all grown up, which Hawk refused to admit. Dayna experienced a momentary qualm when she recalled her brief conversation with Jilly on that very subject. Ruthlessly, she suppressed it. As she'd pointedly reminded Hawk, Gillian Ridgeway was smart. She wouldn't complicate matters by injecting a personal agenda into the mission.

Not that it could get more complicated—or more personal. Where she and Luke were concerned, anyway.

"I should know by tomorrow noon whether I have to pull out of the tournament. If I do, Jilly has my vote as a stand-in on the course. She'll have to jump a plane soon, though, to get to St. Andrews in time for us to bring her up to speed."

Assuming Luke could find his way back to St. Andrews, she amended after she'd terminated the conversation with a still-unconvinced Hawk. Although they'd driven less than forty kilometers, they'd traded the neat towns and fishing villages of the coast for windswept moors cut by rushing rivers and deep glens.

Some five kilometers later the road deteriorated to a dirt track that hugged the shore of the long, narrow loch. Across the lake, the ruins of a castle perched on a high promontory. If there was a hunting lodge anywhere in the vicinity, Dayna couldn't see it.

"Where is this place, anyway?"

"We're almost there."

"How did you find it?"

"It belongs to an RAF colonel at the base. He's invited some of us Yanks out to hunt a few times."

She tried to envision Luke Harper in tweeds with a shotgun under one arm, stalking deer or quail. The tweeds didn't work for her but she had no trouble picturing him as a hunter. In essence, that's what he did every day when he strapped on his two-billion-dollar plane and went after the bad guys.

"The lodge is pretty rustic," he warned, slowing for a tight bend.

Rustic was certainly one way to describe the stone cottage that appeared at the end of the track. A cow byre was attached to one side and the slate roof looked in imminent danger of collapsing in several places, but Dayna had camped out during enough kayaking expeditions to appreciate the fact that it had a roof at all.

On those expeditions, however, she'd toted a knapsack packed with survival essentials. The only essential she carried with her on this outing was the tube of lip balm in her fanny pack.

"I hope the colonel provides his guests with little niceties like soap and/or toilet paper. Or do we go *au naturel?*"

"He keeps the basics on hand."

Luke parked the car in the cow byre and unlocked the front door with a key retrieved from under a loose stone in the windowsill. Dayna started to follow him inside, but a silent vibration against her wrist stopped her in her tracks.

"This is Rogue. Go ahead, Hawk."

"Gillian's hopping a plane tonight," he reported in a voice as stony as the cottage walls. "She'll arrive tomorrow."

Uh-oh. He wasn't happy about bringing in an untrained operative. Neither was Dayna, but she'd rather have Jilly take her place in the charity Pro-Am than anyone else she could think of.

"That was Hawk," she explained to Luke when she entered the hut. "A backup is flying in. I'm meeting with her tomorrow morning."

"You have a treadmill test at nine," he reminded her as he pried open the shutters to let in light and fresh air.

She nodded, looking around. The interior of the one-room cottage matched its rough exterior. The downstairs combined living and eating areas. An open loft constituted the original crofter's sleeping quarters, now supplemented with four metal bunk beds.

Although a gasoline generator could supply electricity, blocks of dried peat stacked beside the stone fireplace were obviously the primary source for heat and light. A bubbling brook behind the cottage supplied fresh water. Nature, Dayna confirmed, would supply the bathroom facilities.

As promised, a metal storage cabinet contained

the basic necessities to include a wide variety of canned goods, tins of tea, soap and tooth powder and an impressive selection of whiskeys.

"All the comforts of home," Dayna drawled, eyeing the array of bottles.

"Did I mention the colonel is a native Scot?"

A rumbling in the vicinity of her stomach reminded Dayna that she hadn't eaten since breakfast. Correctly interpreting the signal, Luke grinned.

"I'm hungry, too. Why don't you kick back and relax while I start a fire?"

"I can help."

"You're supposed to take it easy. Doctor's orders."

Dayna wasn't any more used to being waited on than she was to being hovered over. Embarrassed and uncomfortable with Luke's determined attentiveness, she flapped an impatient hand.

"Opening a few cans won't stress me out. Go start the fire."

Within moments a crackling and somewhat smoky fire chased away the dank smell. Mere moments after that, hearty beef stew sizzled in a heavy cast iron frying pan. Mushing tinned soda crackers with water, Dayna spooned the lumpy mixture into the stew to make dumplings.

Rather than eat at the rickety wooden table, they took their bowls and mugs outside. The late-afternoon sun had warmed the air, although the shadows creeping across the loch presaged an imminent drop in temperature.

Dayna downed her stew with a disconcerting sense of unreality. This morning she'd completed one of the best rounds of golf in her life. Before, during and after the game, she'd been forced to alternate her concentration between her target and her fabricated reunion with Luke. The scary episode at the hotel had upped the pucker factor considerably.

Now, a scant hour and forty-five kilometers later, there wasn't a fairway or green in sight. Just bracken-covered moors, stony crags and a scarlet-breasted kingfisher skimming a few inches above the deep, dark waters of the loch.

And Luke. He was a solid presence beside her, dominating even the spectacular scenery, disconcerting Dayna with his nearness even as she drew a sneaky comfort from it…as she had during those terrifying moments at the hotel.

Gulping, she swallowed her pride with a lump of mushy dumpling. "I didn't thank you."

He slanted her a quizzical glance. "For?"

"For calling the EMTs. For elevating my feet. For, uh, holding me when I couldn't breathe."

Why was that so blasted hard to say? Why did she feel as though she'd just surrendered a part of herself?

Because she *had,* Dayna realized with another gulp. By uttering those simple words, she'd let go of the anger and hurt she'd hauled around for so long.

"It was my pleasure," Luke returned with a smile.

He must have sensed how much the grudging admission that she'd needed him had cost her. His smile tipped into a grin.

"It always was."

She dug her spoon into her stew. "Don't complicate a simple expression of gratitude, Harper."

"You're right. Sorry. Although I have to say *simple* isn't the adjective that comes to mind when discussing your episode this afternoon."

Gut-wrenching didn't come close, Luke thought. *Terrifying* was too tame. He'd let Dayna walk away from him once. The very real possibility she might slip away again, right there in his arms, had shaken him to his core.

Luke would need a thesaurus to find the right words to describe his raw emotions while she struggled for every breath. For now, all he could do was fight to keep his voice light and the memory of her agonized rasping at bay.

He was determined to help Dayna kept it at bay, as well. He could think of a number of ways to accomplish that objective, but only one that didn't involve touching her.

"As I recall, the colonel keeps a deck of cards somewhere in the lodge."

She cocked her head, her competitive spirit stirred. "Cards, huh?"

"Want to play a few hands?"

"Depends on the game."

"How are you at gin rummy?"

"Not as good as I am at kayaking or golf, but I think I can hold my own."

"You're on."

Their few hands of rummy stretched to a duel that lasted into the evening. Rather than power up the generator, they scooted the rickety table closer to the fireplace and played by its flickering light.

Luke didn't let her win. She'd chew him up and spit him out in little pieces if she thought he had. But sitting across from her, watching while she debated over a discard, seeing the sly triumph in her eyes when she snagged the deck, shot his concentration all to hell. As a result, he was both relieved and amused when she gave a little hoot of delight.

"Gin!" Smirking, she slapped down a five-card run to empty her hand. "That's game, set and match, Harper."

Basking in her win, she gathered the cards. Luke hooked an arm over the back of his chair and wondered if she had any idea how beautiful she was. The tough round of golf this morning and the vicious attack this afternoon would have wiped out most ordinary mortals. But Dayna's skin had regained a healthy, natural glow that owed nothing to makeup and her eyes once again sparked with life. She'd released her hair from its ponytail and let it tumble over her shoulders in a tawny fall that made Luke ache to bury his hands in it. Ruthlessly controlling the urge, he exercised his muscle as her self-appointed nursemaid.

"I think we should call it a night."

She flicked a surprised look at the gizmo strapped to her wrist.

"You're right. I lost track of the time. I'll make a quick trip outside and head up to the loft."

He stayed by the fire while she went out. The memory of all the times they'd scrubbed down in Rocky Mountain streams before wiggling into a single sleeping bag stayed with him until she returned.

"You want the top bunk or the lower?"

Luke accepted the unsubtle message that they wouldn't be sharing anything, much less a sleeping bag, with a shrug.

"Your choice. I'll bank the fire and be up later."

Dayna left him in his chair. His long legs were outstretched, his hands threaded loosely over his middle. She would have bet a hefty sum that a prickly awareness of his proximity would keep her awake half the night.

She would have lost the bet. Within the first three minutes of climbing into the lower bunk, she was sawing serious Zs.

Chapter 9

Dayna woke to the trill of a bird perched just outside the only window in the loft. She listened for a moment, smiling at the insistently cheerful song and stretched.

God, she felt great! Rested. Relaxed. Ready to jump back into the game.

Her lazy stretch collapsed. A frown replaced the smile. She couldn't jump back into the game. She'd been sidelined until she completed these damn medical tests.

Crossing her arms over the blanket she'd found in a footlocker, she contemplated the underside of the bunk directly above her. It showed no sagging springs, no half-tucked blanket, no signs whatever of occupancy. Ditto the two bunks on the far side of the room. If Luke had climbed up to the loft last night, he'd slipped in and out with the same stealth as the plane he piloted.

Dayna wasn't quite sure how she felt about the fact they might—or might not—have shared the same sleeping space. Seven or eight hours ago she would have sworn the mere possibility of stretching out in the same room with Luke would keep her wide-awake the entire night. Yet apparently she'd dropped like a stone into the void.

Throwing aside the blanket, she snagged her pants and jacket from the foot of the bed. She'd slept in her briefs, sports bra and stretchy T-shirt. She might just as well have gone commando.

An increasingly urgent need to hit the great out-doors prompted her to strip off the single sheet and army blanket. She left both folded at the foot of the bunk and went downstairs.

Luke was crouched beside the dying fire, coaxing sparks from a peat brick to boil some water. He glanced up at the sound of her descent, and Dayna felt a jolt go through her entire system.

His previously pristine blue oxford shirt was a wrinkled mess. The tails hung out and the sleeves were rolled up over muscular forearms. Stubble shadowed his cheeks and chin. His dark hair stuck up in spikes, as though it had been combed with an impatient hand.

He looked nothing like a spit-and-polish air force officer. Even less like the college senior she'd fallen for years ago. This Luke was a stranger, intent, unsmiling, his face stamped with a hard maturity she hadn't taken time to notice before. Or that he hadn't let her see before.

A sensation that was three parts regret and one part pure sex speared into her belly. If this Luke had climbed the stairs to the loft last night, she might have shed more than her jogging suit.

Both the thought and the sensation brought Dayna up short. It was tough enough cooing and kissing him in public. She'd be crazy to add the complication of sex to the mix.

"I wasn't sure about your friend's laundry arrangements," she said, descending the last few stairs. "I left the sheet and blanket I used on the bunk."

"That's good enough."

Whoa! He sounded as rough around the edges as he looked. That might have something to do with the blanket she spotted lying in a crumpled heap beside his chair.

"Did you spend the whole night in that chair?"

"Yeah. So?"

"Hey, don't jump down my throat. It was your choice."

His eyes narrowed. "Are you saying you wanted me to join you upstairs?"

"No, that is not what I'm saying. But I suggest you try a little attitude adjustment while I go commune with Mother Nature."

With that tart bit of advice, she exited the front door. Cool air scented with the tang of resin and perfumed wood violets greeted her. The spectacular view of the narrow lake and the castle ruins on the opposite side of the lake soothed the feathers Luke's gruffness had ruffled.

Lord, what a setting! Everything inside her ached to walk down to the rocky shore, launch a boat and cut those deep, still waters with the blade of a paddle. She'd have to come back here some day. Maybe after she had the Wus safely tucked away in a safe haven in the States.

Her prickly mood evaporating, Dayna took care of her most pressing concern. She still had some toilet tissue left in her pocket from last night's commune with nature. She'd used leaves and grass often enough, though, that it wouldn't have mattered to her one way or another.

What did that say about her? Dayna wondered

ruefully as she emerged from a screen of trees. Her suite at the hotel offered all the comforts of modern living. Big-screen TV. Jacuzzi tub. Well-stocked minibar. Yet she felt more alive here, more rejuvenated than she would have imagined possible after yesterday's scare.

That was because of Luke, a nasty little voice in her head suggested. She owed him for hustling her away from the reporters. He knew getting back to basics like this would restore her balance. He should. They'd shared so many days and nights in similar outdoor settings.

One more chit to add to her growing debt, Dayna acknowledged. She'd thanked him yesterday for helping her through the attack. She'd have to ignore his foul mood and thank him for this.

Kneeling, she dipped her hands in the stream that whooshed and rippled over rocks on its way down to the lake. Whatever gave Scotland's waters—and subsequently its whiskey—such a sharp, clean flavor was as good as a toothbrush for swishing away all traces of overnight fuzz. She scooped up more water, sloshed it over her face and walked back to the lodge with every pore tight and tingling.

Luke was waiting with a mug in each hand. The strings dangling over the sides of the mugs told

Dayna she'd have to substitute tea for her usual morning infusion of black coffee.

"Is one of those for me?" she asked when he made no move to hand over a mug.

Cursing under his breath, Luke passed her the tea. He'd used to her brief absence unravel the twisted strands of desire and protectiveness that had kept him awake for most of the night.

Yet all it took was one glimpse of her wet, spiky lashes and scrubbed face to tie him in knots again. He hated the thought of driving her back to St. Andrews. Hated, too, the prospect of being relegated to a supporting role while she plunged once more into her mission.

Oh, hell. Who was he kidding? What ate at him from the inside out was the fact that Dayna would disappear from his life again once she and Callahan hustled the Wus aboard a plane for the States. So he wasn't particularly gratified when she cupped the mug in both hands and tipped him a friendly smile.

"Much as I hate to admit it, you were right. I wouldn't have gotten any rest at the hotel. I needed this isolation and quiet."

At least the quiet had worked for one of them. Luke felt like yesterday's garbage.

"Thank you," she said. "Again."

"You're welcome. Again." He didn't know

whether it was the kink in his neck or sheer perversity that made him add a terse kicker. "Although I hope you know I don't want gratitude from you."

"Something tells me I should let that pass. Obviously, you got up on the wrong side of the chair this morning." Angling her chin, she slanted him an assessing glance. "But maybe we should clear the air. Why don't you tell me what you *do* want from me?"

He opened his mouth, snapped it shut. "Damned if I know."

"Liar."

The taunt cut through his layers of frustration and stripped away any attempt at escape or evasion. She'd asked a direct question. He would give her a direct answer.

"All right. I want you."

Her breath left on a hiss, but he took heart from the fact that she didn't upend her mug and dump hot tea over his head. To be safe, though, Luke removed the mug from her hand and set it aside with his.

"Just when did you reach this epiphany?" she asked with more than a touch of sarcasm.

"Last night."

Her expression of polite disbelief goaded him into a full confession.

"I spent half the night reliving those god-awful moments when all I could do was hold you while you clutched your chest. I've never felt so friggin' helpless in my life. The other half…"

Luke shoved a hand through his hair. What idiot had said confession was good for the soul?

"The other half," he continued roughly, "I spent battling the urge to climb those stairs, strip you naked and wipe out any memory but the feel of your mouth and hips locked with mine."

Her lip curled. "So you wanted sex?"

"I wanted *you*. I wanted to bury my face in your hair. I wanted to roll you over and kiss the birthmark at the small of your back. I wanted to hear those little grunts you make when you're about to climax."

"I don't grunt."

"Yeah, you do, Pud. And you send me right over the edge every time."

Yielding to the need that had clawed at him since she walked through the door a few minutes ago, Luke brushed a knuckle over the smooth curve of her cheek. She flinched, but didn't draw away.

"Whatever else we did wrong," he said with an edge to his voice, "we did that right."

Dayna knew she should end this discussion, right here, right now. The problem was, she didn't want to end it. The memories he stirred were too intense and too erotic to shove out of her head. She could almost feel his hands on her naked hips, hear the rustle of the sheets if he rolled her over as he'd just described.

The sensations that had stabbed into her when she'd come downstairs and seen Luke crouched by the fire returned with a vengeance. Her belly tightened. Her vaginal muscles contracted in a tight spasm.

"What if…?" She licked her lips, telling herself this was crazy, willing herself to stop this insanity. "What if I tell you I've been thinking about how good we were in bed, too?"

The light that leapt into his eyes had her planting a quick hand against his chest.

"In bed," she reiterated. "Only in bed. As you said, we screwed up the rest of it."

"We can do better this time," he predicted with a confidence she didn't share.

"Maybe. Maybe not."

She'd offered him her heart once. She wasn't going to lay it out there again. But the strong, fast drum of *his* heart under her fingertips was muddling her thoughts.

"If…and that's a big if…we decided to up ante in this pretend relationship of ours, I'd want to play it the way we sold it to the press. One step at a time."

"Agreed."

He reached for her. Dayna stiffened her arm and held him at bay.

"It would just be sex, Harper. No commitment. No promises."

His eyes narrowed, and for a moment she thought he was going to break off negotiations.

"All right," he conceded after a pause. "We drive back to town. We get you to the cardiologist for your tests. We meet with Hawk. We take care of whatever business needs doing with Wu Kim Li. We deal with the media. Then we have sex. No frills. No hearts and flowers. No promises."

It didn't sound so great fed back to her like that, but Dayna dipped her chin. "Agreed."

When he reached for her again, she folded her arm and got it caught between his chest and hers.

"Just to seal the bargain…" he said, burying his hands in her hair.

This was no kiss staged for the cameras, no skilled performance. This one was raw, elemental. He ground his mouth over hers. The bristles on his cheeks and chin scraped her skin, marking her.

Dayna returned the kiss, holding nothing back. They'd agreed to the terms. Each understood the new rules of the game. She could let go, unleash her hunger for his touch and his taste and his scent. Then count the hours until they made good on their bargain.

* * *

The deal they'd struck occupied a big slice of her thoughts during the drive back to St. Andrews.

It was still early enough that they hit the morning rush hour—such as it was. Vehicles were queued up to cross the stone bridge linking the towns of Leuchars and St. Andrews. The tide was on its way in, churning and eddying the waters of the River Eden as it pushed up the channel. No fishermen or boaters risked the treacherous tidal currents, Dayna noted.

She would have preferred to detour to the hotel to shower and change before her treadmill test but wasn't up to running a gauntlet of inquisitive reporters. Luke delivered her to a side entrance of the hospital, parked the car and talked his way in on her interview with the cardiologist.

"Have you had a nuclear treadmill test before, Ms. Duncan?" the doctor asked.

"No, I haven't."

"It's a quite simple procedure, really. We measure your heart rate and blood pressure at rest, insert an intravenous plug in your forearm and we start you walking. Moderately at first, then with gradually increasing speed and incline."

He paused to hack for a moment. The cough and the pipe stem protruding from his pocket suggested the doc didn't adhere to a healthy lifestyle himself.

"About one to one and a half minutes before you finish exercising, we inject a low-grade radioactive isotope into the plug and flush it with a saline solution to make sure it washes through your blood."

Oh, great, Dayna thought. First she went down like the Berlin Wall. Now she would glow in the dark.

"We'll then place you under a scanning camera to take pictures of your heart," the cardiologist continued. "The images are fed into a computer, which reconstructs them as three-dimensional 'slices.' We let you rest for an hour, and take another series of pictures for comparison purposes. The entire procedure will take approximately two hours."

She didn't doubt her ability to maintain a steady pace, but she wasn't a jogger or long-distance runner. "How long will I actually be on the treadmill?"

"Normally nine to ten minutes, but we'll take you off immediately if you experience chest pains or other discomfort. Shall we proceed?"

Dayna had never thought of herself as a coward. She'd plunged through river gorges, chased a vicious killer through the back alleys of Istanbul and had once fended off an attack by Filipino terrorists. But the prospect of precipitating another bout of agony like the one she'd experienced yesterday made her throat go dry.

"I, uh…"

Luke's hand threaded through hers. Ashamed to admit the comfort she derived from his warm grip, Dayna nodded.

"I'm ready."

After an hour of prep and nervous anticipation, the ten minutes on the treadmill barely raised a sweat. The hardest part of the test, Dayna discovered, was lying absolutely still while the camera made excruciatingly slow passes back and forth across her chest.

After the first series of images, she breezed out of the camera room with a wide grin. Heads turned in the crowded waiting room. Recognition flickered on several faces. Dayna didn't care. She had eyes for only one person.

"Piece of cake," she exulted to a visibly relieved Luke.

"Do you have the results already?"

"Not yet." She plopped into the chair beside his. "They have to shoot the resting images for comparative purposes, but the doc said everything looks good so far. *Very* good."

"Way to go, Pud."

Immensely relieved, Dayna settled back in the chair. She wasn't home-free yet, she reminded herself. That vicious pain had stemmed from something.

Or someone. But she felt more certain by the moment her heart hadn't buckled in on itself.

After studying the various test results, the cardiologist confirmed her self-diagnosis. Dayna left the hospital feeling like a condemned woman who'd just received a pardon.

She was back in the game!

She delivered the news to Hawk after she and Luke arrived at his suite via the hotel's kitchen entrance and service stairs.

"No arterial constriction or aortal anomaly they can determine," she reported crisply. "They'd have to do an arteriogram to assess damage to the actual heart muscle, but the cardiologist is ninety-nine percent confident I didn't sustain any. He wants me to follow up with my doctor at home, though, to try to determine the cause of the attack."

"I think we have it," Hawk replied. "The Edinburgh forensics lab confirmed the presence of a foreign substance in the champagne."

"I knew it!"

"They haven't pinned down the exact substance yet," he advised, his face grim. "They *think* it's an extract of oil from a rare species of orchid."

"I was KO'd by a plant?"

"Not just any plant. This one has a name a mile

long and only grows in a remote corner of Burma. Oil extracted from its leaves is very rare, very lethal when ingested and completely unobtainable in the U.K."

"Burma, huh?" Her glance shot to Luke, zinged back to Hawk. "Doesn't Burma border China? Which in turns borders North Korea."

"Correct on both counts."

An image flashed into Dayna's mind of the masseuse, backed by her array of exotic oils.

"I think I know who might have brought that extract into the U.K." Dayna's mouth hardened. "If I'm right, sumo-mama is going down."

"Sumo-mama?"

"Kim Li's personal masseuse. She looks like a pregnant sumo wrestler on steroids. The woman is right there in the locker room at the clubhouse, waiting for Kim Li after every round with her table all set up. She always has a selection of exotic oils close at hand."

"Looks like we'd better obtain a sample of those oils," Hawk said.

Dayna thought fast. "The first round of the finals kicks off tomorrow. Sumo-mama should set up as usual and wait for Kim Li to finish her round. One pull of the fire alarm will clear the clubhouse long enough for us to gather some samples. Before we do that, though, we should review the hotel's security tapes and talk to people in the kitchen. See if they can verify who had access to the champagne. The director of security… What was his name?"

"Woodhouse," Luke supplied.

"Woodhouse can set up the interviews and tapes."

"I'll take care of that," Hawk said, then pulled up short. "Oh, hell! Gillian's due to arrive in a half hour. I need to meet her, explain you're back on the job and put her on a flight back to the States."

Yeah, right. Like Jilly was going to let that happen. Wishing she could be there to see the fireworks, Dayna waved him off.

"You take care of Gillian. We'll handle things at this end."

She didn't realize she'd automatically included Luke in that "we" until he nodded in agreement.

"Go, Callahan. I'm sticking like glue to Dayna."

Chapter 10

When Dayna and Luke let themselves into her suite, she went straight to the phone.

The message light was flashing. Reporters, she bet, eager to learn the details of her trip to the E.R. Ignoring the flashing red light, she asked to speak to the hotel's director of security.

Woodhouse promised to verify who had uncorked and/or delivered the champagne and make that person available to speak with her. He also promised to review yesterday's surveillance tapes of the kitchen, the wine cellar and the hallway outside her room.

"It might take an hour or two," he cautioned. "The digitized images are fed to our corporate headquarters for storage. I'll have to retrieve them from the server before I can run through them."

"Give me a call when you do."

"I will. And may I say, Ms. Duncan, we're quite relieved to have you back with us."

"I'm pretty happy about that myself."

That done, Dayna dialed for her messages. She had twenty-seven stacked and waiting for her. She listened to the first five or six—all from reporters wanting to know what was behind her trip to the hospital yesterday and why she'd opted out of today's events. Knowing she had to face them eventually, Dayna called the tournament's public-relations director and set up a media conference at 4:00 p.m.

Since it was now only a little past one, that would give her plenty of time to meet with Woodhouse and to take care of the next items on her agenda. They included a shower, a change of clothes and sustenance, not necessarily in that order. Having missed breakfast, her stomach had begun making whiny noises.

"I need to clean up and get something hot and greasy inside me."

"So do I." Luke scraped a palm over his bristly cheeks and chin. "How does fish and chips sound?"

"Like manna from heaven."

"I'll slip down to the gift shop for a clean shirt and razor, then hit the pub next door."

"Think you can appear in public without being waylaid by reporters?"

He palmed his cheek again. "I doubt they'd recognize me with this bush. But I'll take the back stairs, just in case. When I come back, we can work out the details of what we're going to tell them."

There it was again. That ubiquitous *we*. Uncomfortable with how easily they'd slipped into the plural, Dayna backpedaled.

"You've already provided service above and beyond the call of duty. You don't need to hang around here for the media circus."

"Yeah, Pud, I do." He scooped her room key off the sofa table. "You and I have some unfinished business to take care of, remember?"

Oh, sure! Kick every one of her hormones into overdrive and just waltz out the door.

The realization that he'd waltz in again shortly sent Dayna hotfooting it to the bathroom.

She'd fully intended to be scrubbed, brushed, dressed and ready for any eventuality when Luke returned. Unfortunately, she failed to take into account the seductive allure of the old-fashioned claw-foot tub. Combined with the hotel's gardenia-scented soap and bath salts, the prospect of a good soak proved too tempting to resist.

She had at least a half hour before Luke returned with the fish and chips, she reasoned. Plenty of time for a bubble bath. Shedding her clothes, she climbed in while the tub was still only half full.

Ahhh! Feeling every one of her pores open in joyous relief, she slumped against the sloping back. Hot water poured in from the taps. Clouds of steamy fragrance rose all around her. Dayna let the water rise until it threatened to spill over the sides of the tub.

Okay, so maybe she wasn't as dedicated a nature girl as she used to be. She still loved being outdoors, still thrilled to the roar of water rushing through a gorge, still got lost in majestic scenery like that at the hunting lodge.

But this! This was sheer bliss.

Closing her eyes, she sank to her chin in the steamy bubbles. She could have *sworn* nowhere near a half hour had passed when an amused drawl penetrated her sybaritic haze.

"You look like you've died and gone to heaven."

Dayna popped open an eye. Luke leaned a shoulder against the doorjamb. He held a green plastic bag bearing the hotel's logo in one hand. In the other he hefted a brown paper bag shiny with spots of grease.

"That was fast," she commented, resisting the urge to slide lower in the foamy water.

"The pub had butties ready to go." His gaze skimmed her naked shoulders. "Want yours now?"

"You'll have to tell me what a buttie is before I answer that."

"A sort of sandwich. In this case, it's fried cod, chips and curry wrapped up in buttered bread. Scotland's answer to the Big Mac."

Strolling into the bathroom, he dug out a paper-wrapped package and passed it to her. Any doubts Dayna might have entertained about chowing down in the tub vanished when the tantalizing aroma of fried fish and curry overpowered the scent of gardenias.

Peeling back the greasy paper, she eyed the mish-mash of fish, fries and bread slathered with butter. "What is this again?"

"They call it a buttie. Don't ask me why. Go on, take a bite. It tastes a lot better than it looks."

Her first bite confirmed his prediction. The curry added a piquant flavor to the tender, succulent cod. The bread and crispy fried potatoes, oddly, provided a perfect blend of crunch and carbs.

"This is good!"

"You should down a pint or two with it to get the full flavor."

"Too much to do today. I'll make do with tap water."

"That's what I figured."

She thought he would leave her then to feed body and soul. She thought wrong.

"I think I'll join you." His eyes gleamed. "We can have a buttie picnic."

Dayna supposed he'd hunker down on the stool to consume his sandwich. Once again, she was wrong.

Depositing the brown paper bag on the floor beside the tub, he heeled off his shoes. She still didn't quite believe he intended to climb in with her until he popped the top button on his wrinkled blue shirt. Her toes curling, she issued a warning that came out sounding ridiculously breathless.

"You'd better not! You'll waltz around the rest of the day smelling like gardenias."

"I've carried worse stinks. The squadron debriefing room gets pretty aromatic after a crew comes off a thirty- or forty-hour mission."

Mental images of the black, bat-winged B-2 and tired, sweaty crews crowded into Dayna's head, but they couldn't compete with the real-life image when Luke stripped off his wrinkled shirt, jeans and shorts. Her pulse skittering, she recorded the swirls of dark hair on his chest. His hard, flat belly. The corded muscles in the thigh he hooked over the side.

"Scrunch up."

Sloshing water in all directions, he claimed the

opposite end of the tub. His arms looped along the rim. His feet wedged under her hips.

"I think this may be my first ever bubble bath," he commented as the scented foam lapped at his pecs.

"You probably don't want to make a habit of them," Dayna drawled, all too conscious of the toes nudging her butt. "The other crewdogs might get the wrong idea."

His shrug suggested he wasn't particularly worried about his fellow aviators' opinion of his masculinity. Not that anyone could doubt Luke Harper was all male. The proof of that knocked against Dayna's knee when he reached over the side of the tub for his sandwich.

The absurdity of the situation made her shake her head. The hotel's security chief could call at any moment to advise that he'd retrieved the surveillance tapes. Hawk might return from the airport, with or without Jilly in tow. Dayna still had to prepare for the media barrage. Yet here she sat, playing footsie with Luke in a tub of scented water while they gobbled down fish and chips.

"Do you have any idea how ridiculous this is?" she muttered between buttie bites.

Unperturbed, Luke devoured his fish and fries. "Think of it as an exercise in time management."

With his thighs cradling hers, Dayna was having trouble thinking at all.

"We get clean," he said, polishing his sandwich off in a few giant bites, "we fill our bellies, we take care of unfinished business, all in one efficient package."

A gob of fishy bread got stuck in her throat. While she cleared it, Luke tossed aside the paper wrapping from his sandwich.

"You done with that?" he asked, indicating the remains of her lunch with a jerk of her chin.

"I think I've had enough. Luke! Wait!"

Ignoring her shriek, he hooked his hands under her thighs and tugged her onto his lap. Her knees bent at an awkward angle. The remains of her sandwich went flying. She grabbed at the sides of the tub to keep from toppling backward.

"You idiot," she gasped, clinging to the rim while water sloshed over the sides and onto the tiles. "We can't do this now."

"Sure we can."

He slid a hand around her nape and drew her forward. Between sharp, nipping kisses, he reiterated the ground rules she'd laid out earlier this morning.

"You said you wanted to keep it simple. No hearts and flowers. No frills." His teeth scraped her lower lip. "Just old-fashioned, uncomplicated sex."

Sneaky bastard. Tossing the conditions she'd laid down back at her with only a few bubbles separating their naked bodies.

"As long as we agree that's all it is," she returned, all too aware of the hair-roughened thighs under her bottom.

"We agreed to that back at the lodge," he reminded her as his palms cupped her breasts.

So they had. Only Dayna knew damned well there was nothing simple or uncomplicated about the sensations roused by his mouth and tongue and hands. Not to mention the rock-hard ridge of flesh poking her thigh. The feel of him sent a swift punch of desire straight to her belly.

"There's another matter to consider," she said on a breathless note. "Unless you purchased more than a clean shirt and a razor in the gift shop, we don't have any protection."

"Not to worry." Fishing for the now soggy brown paper bag beside the tub, Luke upended it. "I hit the gent's room at the pub."

A rainbow of condoms in different colored wrappers spilled onto the tiles. Dayna knew then she was lost. Still, she took one last stab at reason.

"We'd have to make it a quickie."

Raising a knee, he inserted his hand between their slick bodies. "We'll make it as fast or as slow as you want, Puddles."

Slow, she discovered almost instantly, wasn't an option. The first friction of his thumb and finger against her wet flesh proved that. Gasping, Dayna arched her back and gave him freer access.

Luke took advantage of her vulnerable position to explore at will. She reciprocated by sliding her hand down and wrapping her fist around his straining erection.

They'd made aquatic love before. A good number of times, Dayna recalled with a shiver of ecstasy. In showers. In Colorado's clear mountain lakes. In rivers warmed by late-summer suns.

But never in such a confined space, or with such sudden urgency. Fusing two eager bodies in a narrow tub filled with soapy water that splashed over the sides with every move required a series of athletic maneuvers.

They managed pretty well, considering the hunger that grew with every twist, every touch. This was what she remembered, Dayna thought on spiraling waves of need. This heat. This craving. The old anger and hurt should have eradicated both, or at least diminished them.

Yet every slick of her palms over the hard contours of his body, every bunch of his muscles and rough scrape of his whiskers reminded her she'd never wanted any man the way she wanted Luke. Then, or now.

Grinding her mouth against his, she struggled to get her knees under her. Half the tub had emptied onto the tiles before she sank onto his rigid shaft. Luke reciprocated with a series of upward thrusts that left her gasping. She could feel her climax rushing at her with the force and speed of a runaway locomotive.

"Luke! I can't hold back. We'd better… You'd better…"

Swearing, he pulled out, tore into one of the condoms and sheathed himself.

Dayna groaned and threw her head back. Squeezing her vaginal muscles with every ounce of her strength, she tried to take him with her.

He had other plans. Banding her waist with one arm, he levered them both up. Water dripped from bathroom to bed as he dragged down the covers. Locking her arms around his neck, Dayna took him into her again.

"Wow."

The breathy whisper slipped out as Dayna's sensual haze faded degree by exquisite degree. Flopping an arm over her forehead, she lay sprawled on her back in a tangle of soggy sheets.

Luke's face was buried in the pillow beside her head, his body a deadweight atop hers. When he lifted his head, the whiskers he hadn't yet gotten around to shaving rasped against her upraised arm.

"Yeah," he echoed. "Wow."

She wasn't quite sure she liked his expression. It was one part satisfied lover, two parts possessive male as his gaze skimmed over her flushed face.

"Any time you want lunch delivered to your bathtub, Pud, just let me know."

"I will. Now, I think we'd better get dressed and get to work."

As if to add emphasis to her statement, the house phone buzzed. Dayna reached across Luke's naked chest to snag the receiver.

"This is Victor Woodhouse, Ms. Duncan. I've retrieved the surveillance tapes. The images are best viewed on the high-resolution monitor here in the security center. It's on the ground floor, next to the business center."

"Thanks. We'll be down in ten minutes."

While Luke put the razor he'd purchased in the gift shop to work, Dayna scrambled into clean underwear, gray linen slacks and a short-sleeved silk turtleneck in emerald green that covered the whisker burns on her neck and shoulders. Her hair went into its usual ponytail but, mindful of the media that would descend on her in a few hours, she added mascara and eye shadow along with her lip-gloss.

Not that she needed either. The woman who stared back at her from the dresser mirror showed zero signs that she'd curled up on the floor in agony less than twenty-four hours ago. This woman buzzed with energy and impatience to get on with the task that had brought her to St. Andrews. She also wore the look of a woman well loved.

Whoops. Wrong choice of words. Love didn't constitute part of the equation. She and Luke had agreed on that.

So why did the sight of him emerging from the bathroom with his jeans riding low on his hips make her pulse jump and skip like a barefoot kid trying to cross an asphalt road on a hot summer's day?

Throat tight, she watched him remove the wrapping and pins from the shirt he'd bought in the gift shop and drag the red knit over his head.

"Ready?" she asked when he'd shoved his feet into his loafers.

"Ready."

Woodhouse was waiting for them in the security center. The man took Dayna's hand in his bulldog grip. When he reached for Luke's, his nostrils twitched and a surprised look came over his face.

Dayna bit her lip. Unfazed, Luke supplied the answer to the man's unspoken question.

"Gardenia bath salts."

"Yes, of course. I've cued the surveillance tapes

to an hour before your attack, Ms. Duncan. I think you'll find this sequence very interesting."

With Dayna and Luke at either shoulder, Woodhouse seated himself in front of a flat-screened monitor displaying a frozen image of the kitchens.

"As you may suppose, several of the women competing in the tournament require special diets."

The screen showed what looked like the vegetable prep area of the kitchen, where several cooks' helpers washed fresh fruit and vegetables with an oversized sprayer.

"Miss Wu is especially particular about her meals. Her trainer supplies us with a daily menu designed, he tells us, to provide her with maximum energy and power. He delivered today's menu yesterday morning, an hour before your attack." Woodhouse rolled the tape. "There he is."

Her jaw tightening, Dayna leaned forward and watched the Korean confer with the head chef for several minutes before turning to leave. On his way out of the kitchen, he paused beside a cart containing ice buckets lined up in neat rows.

"The buckets are empty," Dayna observed.

"The bottles that went into them are still in the wine cooler," Woodhouse explained. "But each of the buckets was tagged with a card identifying the recipient and her room number."

"So our friend saw a bucket would be delivered to my suite. But how could he know which bottle would go with it?"

"He couldn't."

Keying in a series of commands, Woodhouse switched to a video showing the length of a hallway. The scene he cued up showed elevator doors opening. A skinny male in his early twenties pushed a cart out of the elevator and rolled it down the hall.

"Do you recognize the waiter who delivered the champagne to your room yesterday, Ms. Duncan?"

"I wasn't there when it arrived."

"I was," Luke stated. "That's him."

"His name is Benjamin Howard. He's a local bloke, has worked for us for three years. He started his deliveries on the second floor and worked his way up. In this sequence, he's delivering a bottle to Ms. Wu's suite. When he knocks on the door, note the time on the screen."

One-seventeen. A half hour after Dayna had come off the course.

"Here he is, exiting Ms. Wu's suite. Again, please note the time."

"One-thirty six," Dayna read. "Almost twenty minutes later."

"After which he took the elevator to your floor and delivered your bottle."

This stretch of video showed Luke opening the door to the waiter. Howard carried the silver tray containing the ice bucket and a crystal flute into Dayna's suite. He exited again a scant three minutes later.

"He stayed inside just long enough to deposit the tray and pocket the tip I gave him," Luke confirmed.

"Back up to the sequence at the doors at Miss Wu's suite," Dayna instructed tersely. "Right there, after he goes inside. Can you zoom in on the cart?"

"Certainly."

Clicking the keys, Woodhouse enlarged the cart until the champagne bottles tipped to the side in their silver buckets looked like a row of drunken soldiers.

"Not one of those bottles is uncorked," she pointed out with a serrated edge to her voice. "Now cut back to the sequence at the door to my suite and zoom in on the bottle."

There it was, larger than life. The silver bottle stopper in the shape of a thistle plugging the bottle the waiter carried into Dayna's suite.

"I want to talk to Mr. Howard."

"So do we," Woodhouse said. "Unfortunately, he didn't show up for work this morning. When I rang up his house a bit ago, his mother indicated he didn't come home last night. She wasn't unduly worried. Apparently he plays on a local rugby team and has caroused all night with his mates before."

"But…" Dayna said with a hollow feeling in her stomach, sensing what was coming.

"But," Woodhouse continued heavily, "none of his mates have seen him, either."

Chapter 11

Dayna received a signal from Hawk as she and Luke were on the way back to her suite. In response to his terse request, they detoured to his room.

When he opened the door, she could see at a glance he was *not* a happy camper. His mouth was drawn into a tight line and what looked like a permanent crease was carved into his forehead.

By contrast, the reason for his sour mood brimmed with energy and enthusiasm despite what must have been a killer flight. Jilly's calf-length suede skirt swirled around her ankles as she rushed across the room to envelope Dayna in a fierce hug.

"You gave us all one heck of a scare, girlfriend!"

"I gave myself one, too. But the docs say I'm good to go."

"Hawk told me."

Jilly's blue eyes raked Dayna from head to toe, as if to verify her condition for herself. Whatever she saw drew her inky black brows into a V.

"You've got some kind of a rash on your neck. Did you show the doctors? It might be a reaction to whatever those bastards put in your champagne."

Dayna took a quick look in the mirror over the console table in the entryway and saw that the cowl of her silky turtleneck had slipped down enough to expose the skin reddened by Luke's whiskers. Shooting him an accusing glare, she tugged up her collar and turned back to Jilly.

"It's not a rash. Just an itchy patch."

When her friend looked unconvinced, Dayna distracted her with introductions. "This is Captain Luke Harper. Luke, meet Gillian Ridgeway. She's currently on sabbatical from the State Department and filling in at the agency Hawk and I work for."

Jilly didn't appear overly impressed by Luke's rugged good looks or friendly smile. Probably because Dayna had let down her guard after a couple of glasses of wine one evening and described how a certain jerk of a pilot had bruised both her heart and her ego.

Gillian shook his hand with a hurt-my-friend-again-and-you-die look in her eyes. Then her expression suddenly altered. Sniffing delicately, she glanced from Luke to Dayna and back again.

"That's a very distinctive after-shave, Captain Harper. What is it? Garden rose? Magnolia?"

"Gardenia."

"Interesting," Jilly murmured, with a speculative glance at her friend.

The exchange baffled Hawk, which didn't particularly improve his mood. He and Jilly must have duked it out royally at the airport. Dayna couldn't wait to get a private report from one or both of them.

"Did you talk to hotel security?" he wanted to know.

"We did."

All business now, Dayna related the sequences she and Luke had viewed on the security videos. She relayed, as well, the grim news that the waiter who delivered the champagne to her room had gone missing.

"No one's seen or heard from him since he finished his shift last night."

"Has anyone contacted the police?"

"Woodhouse said he was going to talk to the mother again and ring the police if she didn't. The guy has been missing less than twenty-four hours, though. They probably won't launch a formal investigation."

"They will once I brief our counterparts in British

Intelligence. MI-6 needs to know about this and the possible source of the orchid extract."

Possible being the operative word. They still had no hard and fast proof the Koreans had supplied the substance or injected it into the champagne. The circumstantial evidence was starting to stack up, however.

"If it came from sumo-mama's bag of tricks," Dayna said grimly, "I'll get a sample. The question we haven't addressed yet, though, is *why* the Koreans would try to sideline me."

She'd been thinking about that. A lot.

"Kim Li's watchdogs have seen us talking. I don't think she was wired but I could have been wrong. If they heard talk of defection, they may have decided to make a preemptive strike."

"That's one possibility," Hawk agreed. "We also have to consider the odds Kim Li knew her conversations with you were being monitored. She and her father could be setting us up to take a fall and make the U.S. look bad in the process."

"There's another consideration," Luke put in. "Dayna burned up the links in the initial rounds. The media were all over her when she came off the course yesterday morning. Could be Tigress Wu decided to pull a Tanya Harding and eliminate her competition."

The same thought had occurred to Dayna. She

knew she wasn't any real threat to Wu, but she'd competed in too many national and international events to minimize the desperation or greed or twisted hopes that drove some athletes. And Wu Kim Li hated to share the spotlight as much or more than she hated to lose.

"Until we know for sure she or her father had a hand in the attack, we have to operate on the assumption they still want to defect."

Hawk nodded. "So we don't let any of the Koreans, including Kim Li and her father, know we suspect them. Speaking of Dr. Wu…" He raked a hand through his hair. "I planned to bend an elbow with him in the bar again this afternoon, but you'll need back-up at the news conference and afterward."

"I'll cover her back," Luke stated flatly.

The two men locked stares.

"You know how to arm and fire anything smaller than a ten-thousand-pound bomb, Harper?"

"I can put a bullet where it needs to go. I'll have to swing by my flat and pick up my service pistol… unless you have a weapon here I can use."

Hawk hiked one leg of his jeans and loosened the Velcro on an ankle holster. "Take this. I'll carry my Sig."

He watched with a professional's keen eye as Luke angled away, slid the snub-nosed .38 from its holster, opened the cylinder and checked the rounds.

"Remington Gold Sabers." Luke snapped the cylinder back into place. "They'll do. What about you?" he asked Dayna. "Are you armed?"

"I am." She patted the fancy designer fanny pack that went everywhere with her. "A Kahr PM40 micro-compact double action."

The realization she'd been armed the entire time they'd spent together put a kink in Luke's gut. He'd accepted the fact that she and Callahan worked for some super-spook agency he'd never heard of. He'd *almost* accepted the danger that obviously came with her job. The knowledge someone had spiked her champagne with a potentially lethal substance fueled a cold, deadly fury in his heart.

"I'll help, too," the black-haired looker who'd just joined their group asserted. "I didn't have time to work a permit to carry a weapon through airport security, but if either of you has another spare I…"

"No way!"

Callahan's flat negative cut her off in midsentence. Unruffled, she met his glare head-on.

"You of all people know I can handle a weapon, Hawk. Or don't you have any faith in your instructional skills?"

"We agreed, Gillian. At the airport. With Rogue back in the game, you're here strictly as an observer. You don't leave my sight while you're in St. Andrews. Or Rogue's," he amended through clenched jaws. "And I'm sure as hell not answering to your father if I let you carry concealed without a permit, here or anywhere else."

"Fine. Then I'll simply provide Rogue and Captain Harper with another set of eyes and ears. What time is this media event, anyway?"

"Four this afternoon." Dayna checked her watch and swore under her breath. "That gives me less than a half hour to bring you up to speed on my contacts with Wu Kim Li. Or has Hawk already done that?"

"He's filled me in on the basics. You and I can talk as we walk."

Slinging her purse strap over her shoulder, Jilly accompanied Dayna to the elevators just across the hall. They left the door open for Luke. While he bent to strap the borrowed .38 to his ankle, Callahan muttered a less than complimentary remark about long-legged, hard-headed females with more brains and beauty than common sense.

Luke jerked his chin up. "Are you saying she's a loose cannon?" he asked sharply. "If so, we don't need her adding to the mix."

"Too bad you couldn't convince Rogue of that," Callahan shot back. "You must have had plenty of opportunity for chitchat, seeing as the two of you waltzed in here wearing the same perfume."

"It's bubble bath, not perfume, and this isn't about Dayna and me." Dragging the hem of his jeans over the holster, Luke rose and hooked a thumb in the direction of the two women. "It's about that blue-eyed bombshell out there in the hall. Is she or is she not a liability?"

"Our boss doesn't think so," the agent ground out. "Neither does Rogue."

"But you do."

"Yes. No. Hell, I don't know." Huffing out a frustrated breath, he shoved a hand through his hair again. "I've known Gillian Ridgeway since her high-school days. As she indicated, I was the one who taught her to shoot. She's smart, she's quick and she has sound instincts on the firing range."

She also had Callahan torqued so tight a hydraulic power wrench wouldn't loosen his screws. Luke could sympathize with the man.

"Guess we'll both have to learn to live with long-legged, hard-headed females."

"Live with?" The other man's glance whipped back to Luke. "You planning to make this temporary arrangement with Rogue permanent?"

"I'm thinking about it."

"Does she know that?"

"Not yet."

For the first time since he'd opened the door,

Callahan's mouth relaxed into something approaching a smile.

"Good luck breaking the news. I've worked several ops with Rogue. She doesn't take kindly to being surprised."

"You handle your woman, I'll handle mine."

Callahan's near-smile disappeared. "Gillian isn't my woman. She's engaged to an Ivy-League type."

"I didn't see a ring."

"It's not official yet, and even if it wasn't…"

He bit back whatever he was going to say, leaving Luke with several unanswered questions.

Not least of which was how the hell he *was* going to break the news to Dayna that he didn't intend to let her walk away from him again. He'd figure that out later. Right now his number-one priority was keeping her alive.

Out in the hall, Gillian was putting her friend through a similar inquisition. "What's happening with you and the studly Captain Harper?"

"It's…complicated."

"Not that complicated, or you two wouldn't smell like identical spring gardens."

Hoping to escape, Dayna stabbed the elevator button. Jilly refused to be deterred.

"C'mon, girl, give! Last time Harper's name came

up in conversation between us, you said something about roasting his chestnuts over a slow fire. When and how did he get a reprieve?"

"He hasn't. Not completely."

"Sure smells like it to me."

Trapped, Dayna threw a look over her shoulder at the two men. "We were playing to the cameras. Pretending a reunion to divert attention from the contacts Hawk and I made with the Wus. We got a little carried away with our roles, that's all."

Jilly heaved a long-suffering sigh. "Do I *look* stupid?"

"Okay! All right! What's between us is as much pleasure as it is business, and that's all you're going to get out of me."

"Until later," her friend predicted.

Luke joined them then, putting an end to that conversation and kicking off another as the doors pinged open on an empty elevator cage.

"If you don't want to tip off the Koreans that we suspect them, what do we say caused your attack?"

"We'll leave it at cause unknown. Could have been anything. Overexertion, a twenty-four-hour virus, an allergic reaction…"

"Too many bubble baths," Jilly offered with an innocent air.

Dayna ignored her. "And we probably shouldn't

label it an attack. More like an episode. I got a little short of breath and we drove to the hospital to have it checked out."

"Don't forget the ambulance crew," Luke reminded her. "The reporters will have ferreted out the fact that they responded."

"Then they'll also know the EMTs didn't provide any medical assistance. I was back to normal—almost—when the crew arrived."

They had the details hammered out by the time the doors open again. The lobby was as crowded as usual. Dayna responded to the questions and concerns of a half-dozen golfers, sportscasters and tournament officials before escaping. Once out on the cobblestone street, she was stopped several times by well-wishers and fans requesting autographs. It was close to four when she, Jilly and Luke approached the Royal and Ancient Clubhouse, standing in majestic splendor just off the eighteenth green of the Old Course.

Dayna remembered the thrill that had raced through her when she'd first spied the stone pillars and chimneys just a few days ago. The prospect of playing the oldest course in the world had ranked a close second to whisking one of North Korea's top nuclear scientists out from under his watchdogs' noses.

The thrill was still there, but tempered by the grim realization that whisking Dr. Wu and his daughter anywhere might prove even tougher than anticipated.

She didn't appreciate how much tougher until the last few minutes of her news conference.

The media center was packed. Seated at a small table, Dayna baked under the intensity of the klieg lights while she responded to the barrage of questions that ranged from general to highly personal and intrusive. Nothing was sacred, from her EKG results to what she wore for the treadmill test to where she and Luke had spent last night.

He stayed off to the side, making no comment when the cameras swung toward him, and left it to Dayna to supply the answer.

"We stayed at a hunting lodge north of Dundee. It's isolated enough that not even you guys tracked us down."

"How did you find the lodge?"

"It belongs to an RAF officer Captain Harper works with."

She made a show of checking her watch. An hour under the lights was enough.

"Sorry, guys, I need to wrap this up."

"A moment, Ms. Duncan," a female with a heavy local accent called from the back of the room.

"Let's talk aboot these RAF officers Captain Harper works with."

Dayna tried to peer through the lights, but all she could see was a figure with a thickened waist and square shoulders.

"I'm sorry, I can't make out your nametag. Who are you?"

"Eileen Brodie."

The woman shouldered her way to the front. In her tweeds and stout walking shoes, she looked like the stereotypical English or Scottish matron out for a pleasant afternoon stroll. The determined set to her several chins said otherwise.

"What media outlet are you with, Ms. Brodie?"

"I report for the *Uplands Daily.*"

"I'm not familiar with that paper? Is it local?"

"Aye. We feed to the *Guardians' Gazette.*"

The stir that went through the TV crews and correspondents raised a red flag. Luke's sudden stiffening also signaled that Ms. Brodie and the *Guardians' Gazette* represented trouble. Dayna switched instantly to damage-control mode.

"I'm afraid I've overextended my time here at the media center, Ms. Brodie." Smiling, she shoved back her chair and rose. "If you have a question for me, perhaps we could talk later at the hotel."

"My question's not fer you, Ms. Duncan." She

zeroed in on Luke. "Is it true yer a bomber pilot, Captain Harper?"

His training, weapons specialty and previous assignments were a matter of record, so he made no attempt to deny any of them. Instead, he treated the woman to a cocky grin intended to defuse the situation.

"I am, and one of the best, I might add, although your Tornado pilots have been teaching me some pretty slick maneuvers during my exchange tour at RAF Leuchars."

Moving to Dayna's side, he grasped her elbow. "We'd better hustle, Pud. You're due at that cocktail party."

"You're right. Thanks, folks." With a smile and a wave, she made for the exit. "I'll see you out on the course tomorrow."

Ms. Brodie didn't give up easily. Pushing past the cameras and lights, she came after them. "Do ye fly a weapon of mass destruction, Captain Harper? Do ye deny there are B-2 bombers at Leuchars?"

Luke dodged the questions with practiced ease. "Come out to the Leuchars' air show next month. We'll have all kinds of aircraft on display."

"The B-2, Captain Harper? Will ye be showin' us the B-2? Och, now!" Scowling, Brodie glared at the woman who cut in front of her.

"I'm *so* sorry." Oozing penitence and charm, Gillian planted herself squarely in the older woman's way.

"Have a care, missie."

The older woman tried to wedge past the younger. Gillian didn't budge.

"I just want Ms. Duncan's autograph. Well, darn," she pouted when the exit door swished shut. "There she goes. I guess I'll have to wait until tomorrow to get it."

Chapter 12

Jilly caught up with Dayna and Luke outside the media center. Her glossy black hair tossing wildly in the wind, she hooked an inquiring brow.

"What was *that* all about?"

Luke explained during the short walk to the hotel. "The Guardians are a group of rabid antiwar protestors. They've designated themselves as unofficial weapons inspectors and have made it their personal goal to uncover and eliminate all so-called weapons of·mass destruction in the U.K."

"Judging by our Ms. Brodie, they sound like a pretty determined group."

"They are. They staged a protest and sit-in at RAF Fairford. That led to a joint U.S.–U.K. decision to base our B-2s here at RAF Leuchars instead."

"The B-2 is that weird, wing-shaped bomber, right?"

"Right. Weird and wing-shaped, with a sortie-reliability rate of just over ninety percent."

"What does that mean in plain English?"

"In plain English, two B-2s armed with precision weaponry can do the job of seventy-five conventional aircraft."

"Hence the objections of the antiwar protestors."

"Exactly. Luckily, the local cadre is small and not as well organized. So far, we've managed to fly under their radar."

"Thanks for running interference back there."

Dayna's comment won a breezy smile from her friend. "Glad I could help. Despite Hawk's low opinion of both my intelligence and capabilities, I don't plan to be a nuisance or get in the way."

Unfortunately, she had to eat those lofty words once back at the hotel.

"I thought the tournament maxed this place out," Dayna remarked as they entered the busy lobby. "I'm surprised you could get a room."

"I didn't. I planned to bunk in with you. That, of course, was before I knew you and Captain Harper had progressed to the bubble-bath stage."

"Luke," he corrected with a completely unrepentant grin.

"Luke," she echoed, her eyes dancing.

Dayna intervened before the discussion deteriorated any further. "You can still bunk in with me. Luke has a flat just across the river, close to the RAF base."

"You sure? I could always camp out in Hawk's suite."

The provocative smile that accompanied the suggestion drew a quick negative from Dayna, but Luke hiked a speculative brow. Interesting. Callahan had sworn some Ivy-League type was close to putting his brand on Gillian Ridgeway. Callahan had also vehemently denied any interest in the woman. Something told him Ms. Ridgeway might put a dent in Hawk's plans—and in Luke's.

He hadn't figured on letting Dayna out of his sight in the immediate future. Although he hadn't formulated specific plans for another session like the one they'd engaged in earlier this afternoon, neither had he discounted the possibility.

Just the thought of tumbling her onto the bed, of nuzzling the soft mounds of her breasts and stroking her long, lean flanks, constricted his breathing. He was contemplating various strategies for palming Gillian off on Mike Callahan when Wu Kim Li sailed out of the public room just off the lobby.

"Dayna! You are here."

Several members of her entourage followed in her wake, including a big, broad-faced female who had to be sumo-mama. The woman's black eyes were unreadable under their heavy folds of flesh as she and the others halted just behind Kim Li.

"We heard you are sick," the girl said, sounding more curious than concerned.

"Something got to me," Dayna admitted with a careless shrug. She didn't so much as glance at sumo-mama.

"You play tomorrow?" Kim Li asked.

"I do."

"Hmm."

The Korean's gaze flicked over Gillian, dismissed her as unimportant and fastened on Luke. Dayna cleared her throat and reclaimed her attention.

"This is my friend. Gillian Ridgeway, Wu Kim Li."

Jilly dipped her chin in a polite nod and rattled off a phrase or two that widened Kim Li's eyes and narrowed those of her handlers.

"How do you learn Korean?"

"I visited your country several times while I worked at the American embassy in Beijing. I know just enough to get from the airport to the hotel and order dinner."

"Ah, so. And how is it you are here now, in Scotland?"

"I've come to watch Dayna play."

Kim Li looked a little put out that Jilly hadn't listed her as a main attraction. "It is good she recovers from her sickness, then."

"Yes, it is."

"I still have a few kinks to work out of my system," Dayna said with deliberate blandness. "I might have to sign up for a massage at the spa." She let her gaze slide past the golfer to the woman standing behind her. "You're lucky to have your own masseuse traveling with you."

Kim Li nodded but didn't offer her assistant's services. Just as well. Dayna's plans for the woman didn't include getting naked around her.

Nor, it appeared, would she be getting naked with Luke. Not tonight, anyway. Suppressing a sharp bite of disappointment, she made for the elevator.

Once back in her room, Luke packed up and prepared to depart but informed the two women he'd return in an hour or so. "I arranged it with Callahan earlier. No room service or banquet food for dinner. I'm taking you both to a place I know. Very quiet, very private, with prime Scotch Buccleuch beef."

Whatever that was. He left Dayna wondering.

He left Jilly wondering, too, but about an entirely different matter. Plopping onto the sofa, she curled her legs under her and pointed an imperious finger at her friend.

"You. Sit. Talk."

Sighing, Dayna sank into the overstuffed armchair. She knew what was coming. Jilly wore an unmistakable, give-me-all-the-gory-details expression. Sure enough, her friend cut right to the chase.

"Start with that hunk of prime *American* beef who just left. And don't try to convince me what's between you and Luke is as much business as pleasure. You've *never* mixed business with pleasure before."

"And I damned well shouldn't be mixing the two now. It…complicates…the op."

"Forget the op for a moment. Talk to me about Luke Harper. From what you told me, he hurt you pretty badly back in the day. Why have you let him into your life again?"

Good question. Dayna wished she had a satisfactory answer. Grimacing, she tugged off the scrunchie holding her ponytail and finger-combed her hair.

"I told you the truth earlier. We started off just playacting for the cameras. Then…well…"

"You got hot, he got hungry and you jumped into a gardenia-scented bubble bath," Jilly supplied when Dayna hesitated. "I can understand that. I'd probably do the same if a stud like Harper offered to scrub my back. Or any other portion of my anatomy. What I don't understand yet is how you feel about him outside the bathtub."

"I wish I knew," Dayna said glumly. "I keep telling myself it's just sex. No strings. No commitments. Exactly as we agreed."

"You negotiated the matter beforehand?"

"Pretty much."

Jilly gave a low whistle. "You're tough, girl. And very smart."

"Make that very cautious. Luke and I went down this road once. Took a long time for the scars from that trip to fade. We both agreed to be more deliberate this time."

"So how's that working for you?"

Dayna dragged a hand through her hair again, twisting the strands into a cable. "Most of the time, I think I'm in complete control, that I'm playing the game by the rules we agreed to. Then Luke will give me one of his damned grins or go into his macho, protective act or feed me butties and…"

"Feed you what?"

"Fish-and-French-fry sandwiches. Local delicacy. You'll have to try one."

"If you say so. Back to Luke feeding you…"

"He does something like that, the rules start to blur and these nasty little 'what-ifs' sneak into my head. What if I want more than a bubble bath? What if I start to tingle at just the sound of his voice? What if a sky flaming with red at sunset makes me ache to share the sight with him? Worse, what if I start to need him again?"

"What if you do? You're not college kids anymore. You're older, wiser and have both achieved success in your chosen fields. Nothing says you can't make a relationship work this time."

"I'd agree, except for one fact. Luke loves the air force and that big, ugly plane he flies."

"Yeah, I kinda got that impression."

"He chose the military over me before," Dayna said with a flicker of the old hurt. "I'm not sure he wouldn't make the same choice again."

Jilly had to stop and think about that. She was on shaky ground here. She'd never fallen for anyone as hard as Dayna had for Luke all those years ago. Not for lack of opportunity, certainly. She'd tumbled in and out of puppy love often enough as a teenager and experienced exuberant passion in college. Her four-year stint with the State Department had also yielded some interesting possibilities, including the dark, intensely handsome Foreign Service Officer who'd served as Charge d'Affaires at the U.S. Embassy in Beijing.

Then there was Wayland Olmstead, the lawyer she'd been dating off and on for the past few months. He kept dropping hints about what a great Washing-

ton couple they'd make, as if that was the be-all and
end-all of his life's ambition. Jilly had told him several times she wasn't in love with him. Wayland,
bless his self-confident soul, honestly believed her
feelings would change given time and the right moves
on his part. All he had to do was chip away at her.

Kind of like she kept chipping away at Hawk, she
realized with a guilty start. She wasn't sure why she
was so determined to make him see her as the woman
she'd become. Or what she'd do about it when he did.
She suspected she'd be just as confused and uncer-
tain as Dayna at that point.

"Does Luke have to choose?" she said after a moment. "Couldn't he—and you—have a career and
each other?"

"Oh, sure. Like that's going to work. With him stationed in the U.K. or Diego Garcia or Guam for a
year at a time, me taking off for parts unknown with
little or no notice."

"You could *make* it work," Jilly argued. "Look at
Nick and Mackenzie. Or my parents. For years
they juggled careers, undercover ops, kids, dogs,
iguanas. And what about the other OMEGA operatives who've made the recent transition from single
to married. Cyrene and Luis? Diamond and T.J.?
Slash and Mallory?"

Dayna conceded the point, but insisted it was really moot at this juncture. "Luke and I aren't any-where close to the transition stage yet."

"You sure about that? He sounded pretty territo-rial a time or two this afternoon."

"That's just the take-charge, macho-military in him."

"You think so, huh? Might be something you two should discuss at dinner."

"We two? Don't you plan to eat with us?"

"I'm planning to crash." Locking her fingers, Jilly stretched her arms above her head. "I barely dozed on the flight over. The time change is catching up with a vengeance. I hate to do this to you, Rogue, but I need to appropriate your bathtub and one of those queen-size beds."

"They're all yours."

The half-timbered posting house Luke had chosen for dinner was on the outskirts of St. Andrews, ad-jacent to the stone bridge that spanned the River Eden. The Romanesque spire dominating the village of Leuchars thrust into the sky on the far side of the river. Water flowed dark and swift between the banks.

The table they were seated at gave a great view of both river and village—and of the RAF fighters glid-ing in for a landing at the air base. The Tornados were mere specks in the sky when Dayna spotted them. Outlined against the swiftly setting sun, their silhouettes grew larger and more distinctive until they sank from sight behind the buildings lining the opposite riverbank.

Once the sun went down, a different breed of aircraft would roll out of their hangars and take off into the night. The reminder of Luke's chosen profession brought her conversation with Jilly forcibly to mind.

Dayna brought it up after the waiter had taken their order for a full-bodied French Bordeaux.

"We haven't had a chance to talk about our, uh, bubble bath this afternoon."

Luke folded his arms on the linen-draped table. He'd spruced up during the quick trip to his flat. His red knit polo shirt and bomber jacket had been replaced with an open-necked shirt in crisp white cotton and a herringbone tweed sports coat.

"Why do we need to talk about it? I thought you wanted to keep things casual?"

"I did. I do. It's just that…"

Dammit! How did she back herself into this corner?

"Casual doesn't always stay that way. Take tonight, for example. This dinner."

She waved a hand, encompassing the linen-covered tables, the flickering votives, the river flowing with the swift, rippling pull of the tide.

"You don't have to romance me."

"Yeah, you made that clear."

He kept his tone light, but Dayna was sure she detected an edge.

"This isn't just for you, Pud. I thought Gillian might enjoy a little local atmosphere. What's the story with her and Callahan, by the way? Does she know she's got the man tied up in knots?"

Dayna snatched at the change of topic. "Did Hawk tell you that?"

"Nope. In fact, he went out of his way to deny it. But he wants her. Almost as much as I want you."

Her breath left on an audible whoosh, but the waiter appeared with their wine before she could respond to the deliberate provocation.

"Are you ready to order?" he asked after decanting the Bordeaux and presenting it to Luke to sniff and swish.

"I am. How about you?" His bland smile told Dayna he knew *exactly* how far he'd thrown her off-kilter. "Want to try the filet of beef? Trust me, you won't regret it."

"The filet it is."

She passed her menu to the waiter along with an order for a house salad and tender white asparagus as a side dish.

"About Hawk and Gillian," she said firmly when he'd departed. "There's nothing going on between them."

"Not yet," Luke agreed, raising his wine goblet. "What shall we drink to?"

He was doing it on purpose, Dayna realized. Deliberately changing directions with every other sentence to keep her off balance. And doing a damned fine job of it, she conceded as she tipped her glass to his.

"Let's drink to the men and women you fly with," she said, thinking of Alan Parks and Gabe and Dweeb.

And Luke, in all his incarnations. The cocky young student pilot who'd had to choose between Dayna and serving his country. The older, more experienced aviator who put his life on the line every time he flew his unarmed bomber into a hot zone. The lover who'd stormed back into her life and stirred up needs and wants she'd thought long dead.

"May you come home safe after every mission."

His eyes grave, he nodded. "Back at you, Pud."

The toast precipitated a dramatic change in mood.

The sexual combativeness and uncertainty that had dogged Dayna since bumping into Luke on the street outside her hotel finally dissipated. He, too, seemed to lose his edge. For the first time, they relaxed and enjoyed each other's company.

Over succulent beef and asparagus so tender it fell off the fork, Dayna learned more about his life and the missions he flew. She opened up about her job at the Outdoor Wilderness Center and shared expurgated details of various ops she'd worked for OMEGA.

The mellow mood stayed with her through the scrumptious dinner, two glasses of wine and a dessert of bread pudding swimming in raisins and brandy sauce. It dissipated fast, however, when they walked out into the starry night and Luke gave her the choice of spending the rest of it at his flat or having him camp out on the sofa in her hotel suite.

"There's a third choice," she countered with a sudden catch to her breath. "I could sleep in my bed, and you in yours."

"Not an option." Cupping her elbow, he steered her toward his car. "I told you, I'm not letting you out of my sight until this is over."

"And then?" she asked as he opened the passenger door for her.

"We reopen negotiations."

The door thudded shut. Luke rounded the rear of the car, slid behind the wheel, keyed the ignition.

"Which is it, Pud? Your place or mine?"

"Yours."

No strings, she lectured herself sternly as she keyed his cell phone and left a message for Jilly that she'd made other arrangements for the night. No complications.

Unless they reopened negotiations.

She knew before she shimmied out of her clothes and straddled Luke's hips there was no "unless" anywhere in the equation.

Chapter 13

The subconscious kindling of nerves and energy Dayna always experienced before a major competitive event woke her just before dawn.

She lay still for a moment, adjusting to the strange bed, the unfamiliar surroundings and the heavy arm draped over her waist. Then the realization that the crucial focus of her mission—getting the Wus aboard a plane to the States—was fast approaching pumped a spurt of adrenaline into her veins. When she tried to wiggle out from under the deadweight, however, the arm tightened and drew her into a solid wall of warm flesh.

"Luke."

She waited a beat and tried again.

"Luke, I need to get it in gear."

A sandpapery cheek rubbed against hers. He mumbled something inarticulate but didn't budge.

"Harper." She added an elbow. "I have a ten-ten tee time."

This time she got a grunt and an irritated grumble. "Plenty of time."

"Not if I want to loosen up on the driving range and spend a little time on the putting green. I need to get back to the hotel, change and collect my gear. Unhand me, sir."

Still grumbling, he eased his hold. Dayna abandoned the comfy cocoon of covers and made for the bathroom. When she emerged some time later, the bed was empty.

Luke's absence gave her a chance to look around. Since they'd had more urgent matters on their minds last night, this was Dayna's first real look at his private world.

The bedroom was typically male—no frills, no fuss: a king-size bed covered with a russet-colored duvet; a leather easy chair; a large-screen TV on a corner stand; functional miniblinds screening the window. A wardrobe stood against the far wall, the mirrored doors ajar. One half of the wardrobe contained civilian clothes. Luke's uniforms took up the other.

Chewing on her lower lip, Dayna surveyed the green Nomex flight suits hanging alongside sets of camouflage BDUs. Next to them was a row of short- and long-sleeved blue shirts, a formal mess dress in a zippered bag and Luke's service dress uniform. The blue jacket displayed rows of colorful ribbons, shiny captain's bars and silver wings. The shelf above held his garrison and flight caps. Highly polished boots and shoes marched in precise order below the uniforms.

But it was the flyaway bag on the floor of the wardrobe, next to the boots, that riveted Dayna's attention. She had only a vague idea of its contents. Aeronautical charts, no doubt. Emergency supplies of cash and medicines in case the crew got stranded at some forward location. Luke's sidearm. Whatever he needed to take off at a moment's notice and remain deployed for long periods.

The discussion with Jilly replayed forcefully in Dayna's mind. Could Luke harness his career so it fitted with hers? Could she do the same?

Did she want to?

She suspected she already knew the answer to that but didn't have time to separate thought from emotion right now. Her tight, controlled energy was mounting by the moment in anticipation of the sporting event to come.

She left the bedroom and glanced into the other two upstairs rooms on her way to the stairs. One doubled as a guest room and office. The other housed a universal gym with an impressive collection of weights and bars and pulleys.

Downstairs, she followed the tantalizing scent of fresh-brewed coffee through a living and dining room. She found Luke in a starkly utilitarian kitchen. He'd pulled on a set of gray sweats and was wielding a spatula like someone who knew how to use it.

"Help yourself," he said, indicating the coffeemaker with a jerk of his chin. "You still restrict yourself to a high-carb meal before competitive events?"

Surprised he remembered after so many years, she nodded and poured life-giving caffeine into a mug. Although golf didn't require the same vigorous energy as steering a kayak through a roaring whitewater, Dayna's training regimen went bone-deep.

"We have buckwheat pancakes," Luke informed her. "We have toasted bagels. We have cereal and whole milk. I think there's some instant oatmeal in the cupboard if you'd prefer that."

"Pancakes and a bagel are more than enough."

"Here you go, then."

Filling plates for her and for himself, he claimed the stool beside hers.

Luke didn't press her for conversation as they ate. He'd shared preevent hours with her before and knew Dayna always narrowed her focus before a major competition. The woman possessed an uncanny ability to tune out everything but the challenge ahead. Most of the time, he'd been okay with that. Looking back, he could chalk up to basic immaturity those few occasions when he'd felt excluded or left behind.

Or was it a reluctance to share center stage in Dayna's life?

Her Olympic dreams had consumed her then, just as his pilot training had demanded all his time and energy. After her coach had called to warn him that Dayna was putting her spot on the Olympic team in jeopardy with her cross-country commuting, Luke believed he'd done right by suggesting they cool things for a while.

Now, he had to wonder whether the suggestion stemmed from a noble desire to see her achieve her goals. Or had there been something less gallant at work? Something small and self-centered, like the realization that he didn't constitute the center of her universe?

If that was part of it—and Luke wasn't ready to admit it was—he'd sure as hell learned his lesson.

All he had to do was look at the woman next to him, see her lost in contemplation as she licked a drop of syrup from the corner of her mouth, and know he'd take whatever part of her she wanted to share with him.

This wasn't the time to tell her so, however. She was already in her zone, already centering on the task ahead with the same single-minded concentration he brought to his preflight mission prep.

"Ready?" he asked when she'd forked down the last of her pancakes.

Blinking, she exited her private space. "I am. Let's do it."

The companionable silence at breakfast proved the last calm before the storm.

As they drove across the stone bridge linking Leuchars and St. Andrews, Dayna could feel her pulse picking up speed and her muscles coiling. The tournament wouldn't win her a title or trophy or a big purse, but cameras would pick up every nuance of her mood, as well as her swing. So would Wu Kim Li. If Dayna and her team were going to pull off the Wus' defection, she had to remain cool and in control.

She managed both through the bustle of a quick shower and change at the hotel followed by a hurried meeting with Hawk and Jilly. After that, she joined her foursome at the clubhouse for a pregame media conference.

Because of their low scores on the initial rounds, Dayna and her partner had the honor of teeing off last, in the same group as Kim Li. The Korean was paired with Joan Ryson-Smith, a tall, lanky South-African amateur who'd inherited millions and played a wicked game of golf. Dayna's partner was the top female money winner on the British women's circuit, Allison Kendall. Short, wiry-haired and intense, Kendall made quick work of the media conference and disappeared to warm up on the driving range. Ryson-Smith watched with amusement as Kim Li hogged the cameras.

That was fine with Dayna. She needed to hit a few buckets, too. Excusing herself, she left the Korean and South African to the limelight and took a short cut through the women's locker room to the club storage facility.

The cavernous, carpeted-and-paneled facility normally buzzed with activity as attendants cleaned clubs, polished shoes and tagged bags before tucking them in their assigned stalls. The caddies, too, usually hung out there while waiting for their players to show and call for their equipment.

With all but the last few foursomes already on the links, most of the stalls were empty. Strange, though, that no attendant manned the front counter. Nor,

Dayna saw with a sudden skip of her pulse, were any caddies milling around inside. ·

That thought had barely registered when a bulky, unmistakable figure emerged from the stall containing Dayna's bag and froze.

The plastic water bottle gripped in sumo-mama's fist carried the Royal and Ancient Clubhouse's distinctive logo…as did the towels, extra sleeves of balls and two additional water bottles sitting next to Dayna's bag. One of those bottles, she noted with a swift narrowing of her eyes, was still filmed with moisture from the cooler. The dew on the other showcased a very distinctive set of fingerprints.

The evidence was unmistakable. Sumo-Mama had dipped into her bag of tricks again.

Enough was enough, Dayna thought with a spear of cold, lethal fury. The woman was going down. Quietly. Unobtrusively. With no one, including Wu Kim Li and her other watchdogs, any the wiser.

"What did you do?" Dayna asked softly, rounding the counter. "Exchange that bottle for one spiked with essence of orchid?"

Recovering from her frozen surprise, the masseuse tried to bluff it out. She shook her head, as if to indicate she didn't understand, and waddled toward the exit. Dayna sidestepped into her path.

"You're not going anywhere, lady."

A gleam of pure malice lit the other woman's eyes. "You stop me?"

"So you do understand English?"

"I understand." Her lip curled. "You move now."

"I don't think so."

Rolling her massive shoulders, the masseuse flexed her arms. She had to weigh a good three-ten or twenty.

"You move, or I crush you."

"Maybe." Smiling coldly, Dayna went up on her toes and balled her fists. "Maybe not."

The ruse worked. Thinking her opponent really intended to duke it out, the other woman smiled in vicious delight, lowered her head and charged.

As nimble as a matador, Dayna danced away and whipped up her arms. She slammed her locked fists down on the back of the woman's neck. The shock reverberated all the way from her wrists to her shoulders.

The karate chop should have brought sumo-mama to her knees. It barely checked her stride. When she turned to charge again, Dayna experienced a decided uh-oh moment.

"You gnat," the masseuse taunted, breathing heavily through her mouth. "I squash you."

Dayna had nowhere to go but into the stall behind her. Her gaze never left the other woman's face as she backed up the few steps. The Korean sneered, lowered her head and charged.

In a swift economy of movement, Dayna plucked the supercharged eight-iron from her golf bag and swung. The clubhead cracked against the Korean's skull. Staggering, the woman grunted once and went down like a felled ox.

"You're lucky I didn't use my driver," Dayna huffed as she tucked the eight-iron under her arm and signaled Hawk. "I'm in the club-storage facility. I need you to dispose of something for me. Better bring Luke," she advised, eyeing sumo-mama's massive bulk.

Keeping a careful eye on the Korean, Dayna searched the other stalls. She wasn't surprised when she found an attendant lying in a crumpled heap. A quick check of his pulse indicated he was alive, but out cold.

Returning to the stall containing her golf bag, Dayna eyed the water bottles thoughtfully. They were capped with plastic tips, the kind you had to pull up before you could squeeze out a squirt of water.

"Perfect."

Planting her butt on the floor, she braced her back against the wall and used both feet to roll sumo-mama over. Groaning, the woman flopped onto her back. Dayna had the water bottle inserted between the Korean's jaws before her lids fluttered up. When the woman saw her opponent poised over her, she jerked convulsively.

"I wouldn't jump around too much," Dayna advised. "Unless you want me to give this bottle a little squeeze."

"Wha…?" Gasping, the masseuse struggled to get her tongue around the spout protruding into her mouth. "Wha' 'ou want?"

"Some answers."

"I know nos-sing!"

"I'm guessing you know how that orchid extract got into the champagne delivered to my room."

"No! No! I… Ay, ah!"

Her brows raised in polite disbelief, Dayna rattled the tip of the bottle against the woman's teeth. When she had her complete attention, she smiled.

"Let's start again, shall we? Why did you try to poison me?"

"Kim Li. She… She…"

"Kim Li what?"

Almost cross-eyed, the masseuse kept her desperate gaze on the bottle wedged between her gaping jaws.

"She—She tell us you say bad things to her."

"What things?"

"You tell her to leave…Korea. Tell her to…be traitor to her country."

Dayna gave no indication that the impetus to leave their native land had originated with the Wus, not the other way around. Instead, she played the heavy.

"Kim Li would make millions in America. Break into the movies if she wanted to. We can make her the international superstar she should be."

"Money no matter. Kim Li never leave Korea. Never leave mother."

Tight-jawed, Dayna jammed the bottle almost to the woman's tonsils. "Her mother's dead."

"No!" the masseuse got out between gagging gurgles. "Mother alive. Held by government."

"So you made the girl choose between her mother and her father? He skips, she stays."

"Dr. Wu no traitor! Just—Just pretend. Learn secrets. Bring back to Korea. Return to wife."

So neither of the Wus had really intended to defect. The realization that they'd played Dayna and Hawk like twin accordions made her ache to give the bottle's plastic sides a teensy-weensy little squeeze.

"Rogue! What's going on?"

Hawk rushed into the storage facility. With a twinge of real regret, Dayna sat back on her heels. The stall was cramped enough with just her and sumo-mama. When Hawk, Luke and Jilly crowded in, she barely had breathing room.

"This is Kim Li's masseuse. She didn't care for my attempts to proselytize her protégée and decided to flavor my drink. Again."

Extracting the water bottle from the woman's

mouth, Dayna tipped it upright. The plastic cap was still firmly in place.

When the Korean realized she'd never been in danger of swallowing any of the tainted liquid, she gave a bellow of pure rage.

"You lie!" Her bulk heaving, she struggled upright. "You lie like dog."

Dayna tossed the bottle into her other hand, hefted the eight-iron again and swung. The woman dropped like a stone.

Jilly's blue eyes rounded. "You don't mess around, do you?"

"Not with someone who tried to poison me." Swiftly, she related the gist of the masseuse's revelations. "Here, Hawk. Have the lab analyze this water. I think it'll provide sufficient justification for the Brits to keep sumo-mama on ice until the tournament's over."

"What do we gain by keeping her on ice? From what you just told us, neither Kim Li nor her father wants to come over to our side."

"The Wus don't know *we* know that." Dayna bit her lip, trying to sort things out in her head. "And *we* don't know for sure Kim Li's mother is still alive. All we have is mama-san's word for that. We need to get hold of Lightning and see what our people in Asia can ferret out about Madam Wu."

"I'll take care of that," Jilly volunteered. "I have a few contacts in Asia that might prove useful."

With that piece of the puzzle taken care of, Dayna mulled over the outrageous plan taking shape in her head. Her glance zinged to Luke.

"Dr. Wu's mission is to ferret out America's nuclear secrets," she said slowly. "What do you think? Could we feed him some?"

"Depends on what you have in mind."

"We're taking him to the base for transport. What if he saw some things he wasn't supposed to? Some things that might give him and his pals a false idea about our own nuclear-weapons program?"

"You mean, we should feed him deliberately erroneous information about the B-2?"

"Something like that?"

"It might work." His brows slashing, he considered the possibilities. "Hell, we'll *make* it work."

"You guys discuss it while you haul sumo-mama's carcass out of here. I've got to hustle to make my tee time. Oh, and check the bag boy in the stall over there. I think he's okay, but I suspect he'll have the mother of all headaches when he wakes up."

Adrenaline surging, Dayna hooked the strap of her golf bag over her shoulder. Its familiar weight bumped against her hip as she exited the storage facility into the bright, sunlit morning.

The other three had already gathered in the hot zone with their caddies, awaiting the call to the first tee. Dayna's partner looked relieved to see her. Kim Li's partner smiled a greeting. The Korean, however, scowled and sliced her driver back and forth across the grass.

"You late."

Was she aware of her muscle-bound masseuse's plans to spike the water bottle? If so, she hid it well behind a mask of pouty impatience.

"Sorry 'bout that," Dayna said easily. "Anyone know what happened to my caddie?"

Kim Li raised her driver and stabbed it at the short, bowlegged Scot hurrying toward them. "He's there."

The bandy-legged local huffed up. Pouring out apologies, he identified himself as Angus MacDougall as he relieved her of her bag.

"I'm verra sorry, Ms. Duncan. They told me you were waiting for me at the clubhouse. I don't know how the signals got so crossed."

She had a good idea. Hawk and Luke were no doubt piling the crossee into a golf cart as they spoke.

"No problem," she said, smiling to put him at ease.

Clearly upset, he hoisted her bag over his shoulder. "I hope this doesna throw you off your game."

"It won't."

The utter confidence in her reply deepened Kim Li's scowl. Notoriously temperamental and impatient before a game, Tigress Wu didn't handle delays or miscues well.

"They call us to the tee. We play now."

Chapter 14

The suspicion that Wu Kim Li didn't really intend to skip to the States freed Dayna from the necessity of catering to the girl's ego on and off the links.

A sizzling, crackling energy coursed through Dayna's veins as she waited her turn on the first hole. Off to her left, the ancient buildings and chimneys of St. Andrews looked down on the course. To her right, the leaden waters of St. Andrews Bay lapped at marshy shores.

Dead ahead lay the Old Course, with its savage gorse, monster double greens and one hundred and twelve bunkers that included the infamous Hell on

the fourteenth hole, Strath on number eleven and the
Road Bunker on number seventeen—probably the
most famous hole in all golf.

The first hole was three hundred and thirty-nine
yards of flat, barren fairway. Flat, that is, until the
Swilcan Burn, an undulating loop that guarded the front
edge of the green. Joan teed off first, whacking her ball
far right and dangerously close to out-of-bounds.

Kim Li clicked her tongue at her partner's inaus-
picious start. The Korean was dressed in black today.
Her slacks, stretchy turtleneck, windbreaker and visor
were all in sleek ebony that prominently displayed her
sponsor's logo done in gleaming gold.

Ignoring her caddy's offer of assistance in reading the fairway slope, she teed up and took a couple
of practice swings before exploding in a perfect fusion of grace and power.

"Nice shot," Dayna commented, exchanging
places with the girl.

They couldn't have made more of contrast, she
thought as she loosened up with a practice swing.
Small, delicate Kim Li with her black hair, black eyes
and black uniform. Dayna, taller, blond, wearing the
bright colors she preferred—glowing, jewel-toned
amethyst slacks and windbreaker, a white silk turtleneck, a ball cap studded with iridescent spangles.

Their stance and swings were almost identical,

though. Feet spread to shoulder width. Ball forward. Slow and steady on the backswing. Rocket speed and power on the downswing. All weight on the left foot at the finish.

A roar from the gallery signaled their approval when Dayna's drive rolled to a stop just left of the fairway's center, mere inches from Kim Li's.

"Yes!"

The normally reserved and intense Allison Kendall gave her partner a high five and stepped onto the tee box. She, too, powered her drive.

The chase was on.

It took the foursome just a little over two hours to reach the midpoint of the match. Dayna and Allison both posted a two-under par at the turn. Kim Li came in at a blazing four under. Since her partner's handicap was three strokes higher than Dayna's, Wu and Ryson-Smith had a solid lead.

Not for long, Dayna vowed while she waited her turn on number ten. Hands crossed on the rubber grip of her driver, she searched the gallery.

She'd spotted Dr. Wu earlier. Bundled against the breeze in plaid Burberry scarf and jacket, he'd followed Kim Li's foursome from hole to hole. Two of his countrymen stuck close to his elbow.

Jilly had joined the gallery ringing the tee box.

Her glossy, wind-tossed hair made her an easy stand-out. Her gleeful grin and thumbs-up conveyed support and encouragement to the casual observer. To Dayna, they were a signal that Luke and Hawk had succeeded in dumping sumo-mama into the loving arms of the British authorities.

Sure enough, Hawk strolled out of the clubhouse just as Dayna prepared to tee off. She acknowledged his presence with a nod. He returned it, looking relaxed and sporty in a flat-billed tweed cap. By the time the group had reached the green, Hawk had struck up a seemingly idle conversation with his drinking buddy, Dr. Wu.

The only missing member of their team was Luke. Dayna felt his absence more than she'd expected to. She knew he'd raced back to RAF Leuchars to explore the wild scheme she'd suggested. He was probably locked away with his detachment commander at this very minute, trying to figure out whether it was possible to feed one of North Korea's foremost scientists misleading and totally inaccurate information about the United States's nuclear-weapons program.

So she shouldn't miss seeing his broad shoulders and easy, hands-in-pocket stance in the gallery. Or wish he'd witnessed her spectacular bunker shot on number five. And she sure as hell shouldn't be thinking about a private, posttournament celebration that might or might not involve butties!

"Focus, Duncan," she muttered, shoving the image of a naked, sweat-slicked Luke out of her head. "Focus."

The back nine tested the skills of each member of the foursome to the max.

Allison went out of bounds on ten. Joan got trapped in Strath Bunker on eleven and needed three strokes to climb out. Kim Li bogeyed twelve *and* thirteen. Dayna hit the nasty clump of bunkers known as the Beardies on fourteen, but managed to save par.

By the time they teed up on fifteen, Kim Li's temper was manifesting itself with a vengeance. After each less-than-perfect swing, she thumped the ground angrily with her club before shoving it at her caddy and stalking off. The cameras caught her berating a spectator who pressed too close to the ropes. Supersensitive microphones recorded curses in both Korean and broken English.

World-famous number eighteen almost proved the straw that broke the camel's back. Technically, eighteen wasn't that difficult a hole. Three hundred and forty-two yards straight to the Royal and Ancient Golf Clubhouse. The challenge came in the form of Swilcan Bridge, spanning the creek that snaked through the fairway and the Valley of Sin that guarded the green.

Kim Li powered her drive, but it went low and smacked into the stone bridge. Zinging away at a sharp right angle, the ball flew across the road, ricocheted off the roof of a passing car and shattered a plate-glass shop window.

"Out of bounds," the course official intoned solemnly while the gallery burst into cheers and laughter.

Furious, Kim Li slung her club at her caddy. The laughter died. A few scattered boos came from the normally decorous gallery as the disapproving course official delivered a stern warning.

"Here now, Miss. We'll have no more of that."

The chastisement did little to improve Kim Li's mood. It deteriorated even further when the foursome holed out, and Dayna and Allison's combined scores topped the leaderboard. Kim Li and her partner ranked second, which meant they'd make up the same foursome again for the last round of the tournament.

"We play again tomorrow," the Korean acknowledged with a distinct lack of enthusiasm. Her obligatory handshake was curt and forced.

"So we will," Dayna agreed blandly. "Tomorrow will be a big day—in more ways than one."

With so many people milling around, she didn't dare make more than a veiled reference to the Wus' supposed desire to escape to the States after the tournament.

Even that subtle reminder was enough to wipe the temper from Kim Li's face. Her glance darted left, then right. For the barest fraction of a second, uncertainty darkened her eyes. Or was that fear? It came and went so swiftly, Dayna couldn't decide.

During the brief pause, unanswered questions rolled around inside her head like loose ball bearings. How far would the Wus go with their double deception? Was the daughter merely playing along until the father actually boarded a plane to the U.S.? How did Dr. Wu plan to leave the States once he'd gathered the information he'd been sent to collect? Was Kim Li's mother really alive and being held as surety for her husband and daughter's return to Korea, or was that, too, a lie?

"Perhaps we should discuss tomorrow's agenda," Dayna suggested, reminding the teenaged superstar that they hadn't yet confirmed the details of the escape.

"Yes," Kim Li muttered. "We must discuss tomorrow."

With the Korean's trainer and manager swiftly converging on their protégée, Dayna thought fast. Any meeting outside the scope of the tournament would raise instant suspicion. Best to do it in the open, under the guise of a business-slash-social event.

"As you may know," she said loudly enough for Kim Li's handlers to overhear, "I work for the largest outdoor recreation training facility in the United States. We're in the process of organizing a one-time mega event to promote health and fitness among kids. We've lined up a host of international sponsors and extensive media coverage. I'd like to talk to you about participating. Perhaps you—and your father, of course—could join me for dinner this evening?"

"Dinner. Yes." Kim Li glanced to the left, received an almost imperceptible nod from her trainer. "Will Captain Harper also come?"

"Luke?"

"My father has heard… That is, he's seen rumors in papers about this plane the captain flies."

Dayna just bet he had! If she'd needed any further verification of the Wus' intended duplicity, Kim Li had just handed it to her.

"I'll invite Captain Harper to join us. The hotel dining room, seven o'clock?"

Dayna hoped Luke would be back by then. She needed him in on this meeting. She also needed to know whether they could pull off the wild scheme they'd hatched earlier.

"My father and I will be there," Kim Li confirmed.

Dayna relayed the dinner engagement to Luke by phone, wondering how had he become such a vital part of her op. And her thoughts, dammit. The man had been in her head, if not in her direct line of sight, throughout the entire day. He promised to make the appointment, but didn't have time to brief her on his activities until he made it back to the hotel.

When he arrived at her room at six-twenty, he would have appeared cool and in control to a casual observer. Dayna's antennae had become so resensitized to the man, however, that one glance at the glint of excitement in his eyes kicked her pulse into overdrive.

"Tell us," she demanded as he shed his jacket and tossed it over the back of a chair.

"We had to go all the way to the top brass at the Pentagon but we got the green light for what could be the scam of the century."

Too revved to sit, he paced the sitting room and laid out a hastily contrived, incredibly complex scheme for Dayna, Hawk and Jilly.

"As soon as we got the go-ahead, Colonel Anderson activated a total detachment recall. Our ground crews and contractors are already fabricating fake engine cowlings, cockpit shields and wing mounts for one of our birds.

"The changes will be so subtle no one except a B-2 crewdog could detect them, but they'll alter the aircraft's radar signature enough to return an erroneous signal. We'll arrange for Dr. Wu to get a glimpse of the modified bird through the hangar doors when you take him to the aircraft that's supposed to transport him to the States. If his people outfit him with a hidden camera or digital-imaging device…"

"We have to assume they will," Dayna said.

"Then he'll transmit some very precise, very false images of the B-2."

A savage satisfaction roughened Luke's voice as he described the furor of activity occurring at the base.

"We're also scrambling to concoct an altered formula for the radar-absorbent coating we spray on the skin. The plan is to let Dr. Wu pocket a minute sample of something sprayed with the fake coating. The North Koreans will blow their supercomputers trying to reverse-engineer the altered formula and figure out how the hell to get it to stick."

"What about nukes?" Hawk asked. "Those are Dr. Wu's specialty. He knows the B-2 is nuclear-capable, although it's more than proven its worth by delivering conventional munitions in the current conflict. You planning to blow smoke up his ass about that, too?"

"We're sure gonna try. In fact, we figured we'd kill two birds with one stone."

Luke's manner, his stance, his energy all conveyed a single, intent focus. He'd unleashed his hunting instincts and had locked on his prey.

They were so much more alike than she'd been

willing to admit, Dayna thought as an answering thrill shivered down her spine. Both hunters, both zeroed in on their mission. A well-matched pair, she acknowledged silently.

"Colonel Anderson and I decided to let our friend, Ms. Brodie, feed the good doctor and his pals a treasure trove of misinformation."

Dayna and Jilly gaped in surprise. Hawk, who'd missed Ms. Brodie's harangue during the media conference yesterday, had to be reminded of who she was.

"Hold on a minute," he protested. "Are you saying Colonel Anderson and the Pentagon brass have decided to reveal the B-2's presence at RAF Leuchars to a bunch of rabid antiwar activists?"

"Not quite. One of our crewdogs, however, will down a pint too many tonight at a pub regularly frequented by several of these activists." His glance caught Dayna's. "Alan Parks has volunteered for this dangerous mission, by the way."

"Why am I not surprised?" she drawled, recalling the pilot's cocky assertiveness. "What happens after he gets inebriated? Or appears to?"

"He'll act confused and swear he didn't so much as mention nukes *or* a plasma separator."

"Who or what is a plasma separator?"

Luke's grin was swift and predatory. "It's a technique developed by the French that uses superconducting magnets and plasma physics to enrich uranium. The North Koreans are desperate to obtain enough U-235 to fuel their weapons-development program."

"Can they get it from this plasma separator?"

"They can, *if* they manage to beg, buy or steal the technology. Even then it would take decades to bring the separator to full production capacity. We tested the process a few years ago, incidentally, but didn't find it either efficient or cost-effective. Dr. Wu knows that. Or thinks he does. Ms. Brodie might convince him otherwise, particularly when both the U.S. and the U.K. flatly deny the existence of both a storage site and a separator."

"Which do not, in fact, exist," Dayna finished with an answering grin. "Making Ms. Brodie and company look *extremely* foolish when they troop through acres of gorse and heather looking for both. Neat. Very neat."

"We think so," he said smugly.

"You work fast, Harper." She couldn't believe he'd pulled everything together so with such speed and precision. "Think we can carry this off?"

"We'll sure give it a helluva try, Puddles."

"Puddles?" Jilly echoed, amusement lighting her blue eyes.

"I'll explain later," Dayna lied with a quick glance

at her watch. "Luke and I need to get down to the restaurant. We don't want to keep our guests waiting."

Nodding, Jilly waited until the door closed behind them. Then she treated Hawk to a look of wide-eyed innocence.

"Looks like it's just the two of us for dinner."

Dayna and Luke beat the Wus to the dining room by a scant couple of minutes.

The Koreans' watchdogs were already seated at another table some distance away. Kim Li's trainer flicked a glance in Dayna's direction as the hostess seated her. His expression gave no hint of his thoughts, but he had to be aware of sumo-mama's disappearance by now. Did he suspect Dayna and Luke of engineering that? Did Kim Li?

The girl's pale, strained face when the hostess led her to the table a few moments later suggested she did. Dr. Wu looked almost as tense as his daughter. Perspiration beading on his cheeks and forehead, he shook hands with Luke before taking his seat.

"I have read of you in the newspapers," he said in heavily accented English. "You are a pilot, yes? With the American air force?"

"I am."

"I, too, wore uniform of my country. Many years ago. Now only humble scientist."

"You're too modest, sir. I've read the paper on fusion you presented to the Twenty-Eighth International Congress of Nuclear Scientists. That was anything but humble."

Good grief! Luke *had* been busy. Did he dig up that presentation this afternoon, between arranging for the fabrication of fake skin for his aircraft and setting up Ms. Brodie's gang for a fall?

A silent, sneaking admiration added to the combustible mix of emotions Luke Harper had already stirred in Dayna's heart. The smart, handsome college senior she'd fallen for all those years ago didn't compare to the smart, handsome, self-assured officer he'd become.

"Why you read my paper?" Dr. Wu asked after a quick look over his shoulder.

The brief, almost furtive glance didn't fool Dayna. The Wus had to be wired. Their watchdogs wouldn't let them out of earshot unless they could monitor their conversations.

Shrugging, Luke played to the hidden mike. "Let's just say I have an interest in the subject."

Removing his glasses, the scientist polished them with great care. When he put them on again, his face had lost every trace of color. Kim Li wasn't in much better shape. She had her napkin bunched in a white-knuckled fist.

"Perhaps…" Dr. Wu cleared his throat. "Perhaps we talk more on this when Kim Li and I come to base tomorrow."

"That can be arranged."

Luke didn't so much as twitch a facial muscle, but Dayna could sense the same intense elation in him that almost made her squirm in her seat.

The Koreans had taken the bait.

Sweating in earnest now, the scientist mopped his forehead with his napkin. "How we go to base?"

Dayna used her menu to hide her mouth from any astute lip-reader. She had to play the game.

"My associates, Mike Callahan and Gillian Ridgeway, will separate you from your watchdogs during the hubbub immediately prior to the trophy presentation. Do you remember Gillian? You met her yesterday."

"The woman who speaks Korean?"

"That's the one. She and Mike will take you to the aircraft that will transport you to the States. Luke and I will bring your daughter."

Kim Li wadded her napkin into a tight ball. "Can my father and I not go together?"

Not if they wanted to give Dr. Wu time to observe the altered Stealth bomber without raising suspicions.

"It's best if we take two vehicles. We've arranged tight security for both."

Father and daughter shared a glance. Then he gave an almost imperceptible nod.

The crumpled napkin slid off Kim Li's lap. She bent to retrieve it before the waiter could come to her assistance. Using the tablecloth skirting as a cover, she dropped a folded slip of paper into Dayna's lap.

Casually, so casually, Dayna unfolded her own napkin and draped it over her lap.

Chapter 15

"The Wus want a helicopter hovering a half mile from a specific point along the DMZ at twenty-three hundred tomorrow, Korean time?" Lightning's glance shot to the bank of clocks on the far wall of the Control Center. "That'll be 3:00 p.m. there in St. Andrews."

"Roger that." The Control Center's sensitive speakers amplified the quiver of excitement in Rogue's voice. "Just about the time the tournament is expected to wrap up. The note cites the exact coordinates."

As she rattled off the latitude and longitude,

OMEGA's on-duty controller punched them into his computer. Instantly, the digitized map of the Korean peninsula projected onto the wall-size screen enlarged.

The Demilitarized Zone went from showing as a thin scar across the middle of the Korean peninsula to a fat strip marked with observation posts on both sides every hundred yards or so. Interspersed among the guard posts were several narrow, snaking lines that bisected the DMZ.

"Hang on, Rogue."

Squinting, Lightning tried to decipher the unidentified lines. Since all traffic between North and South was strictly controlled at the main checkpoints, they couldn't represent roads or rail tracks.

"Zoom in on that line on the left," he instructed the controller.

The satellite imagery sharpened to display incredible detail. So precise that Lightning could see a goat grazing dangerously close to the barbed wire that enclosed the heavily mined DMZ.

"Well, damn," the controller muttered, zeroing in on a shadowy blur. "That looks like the opening to a tunnel."

"It is," Lightning confirmed with sudden recall. "An infiltration tunnel, dug by the North Koreans a half century ago."

"Come again?" Rogue asked via the speakers.

"Years ago North Korea dug a series of tunnels under the DMZ in preparation for an invasion. The invasion never happened, and an engineer who defected in the late seventies revealed the tunnels' existence. The South Koreans uncovered four. Each was more than two kilometers long and wide enough to allow passage of an estimated thirty-thousand troops per hour. The defector claimed more than twenty had been dug. If so, they're still well hidden."

Now, apparently, another defector intended to use one of those hidden passages as an escape route.

"Does the note say who the helicopter is supposed to pick up?"

"Negative," Rogue replied. "Only that she'll flash three short bursts of light and one long as a signal for them to come in."

"She? The note specifies a 'she'?

"It does. We—Hawk and Luke and Jilly and I— think it must be Wu's wife."

"We haven't received confirmation from our contacts in Korea that Madam Wu is alive," Lightning cautioned.

"True. We're going with our collective gut here, backed up by the masseuse's stuttering assertion."

"And your gut says Dr. Wu has arranged his wife's escape and is using us to make it happen."

"Exactly. We're guessing the doc and his daughter will hedge their bets and demand proof she's safe before they climb aboard a plane at this end."

Lightning shoved back his suit jacket and thrust his hands in his pockets. He'd attended a meeting at the White House only a few hours ago. Relations between the U.S. and North Korea had gone well past strained and were edging toward hairy over Pyongyang's determination to build a nuclear arsenal. The President was determined to put a spike in North Korea's program by aiding Dr. Wu and his daughter to defect. Now, apparently, they'd added a third person to the equation.

"We can relay a radio transmission if and when the chopper crew picks her up," Lightning assured his field agent. "But I have to say, everything about this op gets more squirrelly by the hour."

"No kidding! Can I confirm with the Wus the chopper will be at the designated rendezvous point?"

Squirrelly or not, Nick didn't hesitate. The U.S.— hell, the world—had too much at stake.

"You can."

Across the Atlantic, Dayna ended the transmission and faced her three coconspirators. Empty cups and Pellegrino bottles littered the coffee table. Hawk, Jilly and Luke's expressions reflected the same combination of doubt and cautious optimism she suspected hers held.

"So we stick to the game plan?" Luke queried. "Hawk and Jilly take the doc, you and I escort Kim Li?"

"Unless you think you should be the one to show Dr. Wu around the base."

"Colonel Anderson has that covered. I do need to head back to Leuchars tonight, though. I want to hear how Alan Parks' visit to the pub went and make sure everything is a go for tomorrow."

Tomorrow was taking on more twists than a boa with rickets, Dayna thought. After looking at their scheme from every angle, however, she was still convinced they should go through with it. If Dr. Wu's real intent was to spy for his country, he'd absorb and—hopefully—feed his cohorts completely false information. If he *did* plan to go over to the West, he could still feed the North Koreans false data right up to the moment he boarded the plane to the States.

It sounded, smelled and tasted like a win all around for Dayna and her team. She'd feel a lot more confident if they didn't have to contend with so many damned "*if*s."

"I'll go with you," Hawk said. They'd hashed and rehashed the game plan so many times every detail was burned into their brains. They all needed a break. More to the point, he needed to put some distance between himself and Gillian. Three solid hours in her company had brought him too damned close to forgetting all the reasons he was wrong for her.

"My car is in the parking lot behind the hotel." Luke shepherded the women to the door. "I'll see the ladies to their room and meet you downstairs."

"We can probably make it up one floor on our own," Dayna commented at the elevator.

"I'm sure you can." Unperturbed, he hit the button. "We need to settle another issue before I hit the road."

"Another issue?" She wracked her mind while the elevator winged up one short flight. "What string did we leave dangling?"

"This one's personal."

The offhand comment was enough to trigger a swift mental leap from fifty-year-old invasion tunnels and plasma separators. That, and the hand Luke hooked around her arm to detain her when they entered her suite.

"You mind, Jilly?"

"Not at all."

Waggling her fingers, Gillian steered a straight course for the bedroom. Dayna's heart was thumping before the door closed. She had a good idea now what issue he wanted to settle. Luke confirmed her guess with a gentle stroke of his thumb along the inside of her arm.

"We may not have time tomorrow, so I thought we'd better reopen negotiations tonight."

"We don't have much time tonight, either, with Hawk waiting for you downstairs."

"It won't be a complicated negotiation. I lost you once, Pud. I don't want to lose you again."

The simplicity of it took her breath away. And left no room for anything but the truth.

"I don't want to lose you, either."

"That's all I needed to hear."

Tugging her into his arms, he covered her mouth with his. Dayna returned the kiss, holding nothing back. She had no idea where they'd go from here. For the moment, this was enough. More than enough, she thought when Luke raised his head and smiled down at her.

"My active-duty service commitment is up in four months. If I take terminal leave, I'll be back in the States in three."

"Terminal leave?" Startled, she blinked up at him. "Are you talking about quitting the air force?"

"We tried long-distance love once. It didn't work. I'm not taking any chances this time around."

"But…"

"No buts. We can't make a life together on separate continents. End of negotiations."

His mouth descended on hers again, more fiercely

this time, before he left with a parting admonition. "Lock the door behind me."

She did as instructed, feeling more than a little shell-shocked. And she thought Wu Kim Li had dropped a bomb in her lap!

Luke and her, making a life together.

On one continent.

After he separated from the air force.

All these years Dayna had resented the fact that Luke had put his military career ahead of her. So why did his abrupt decision to hang up his uniform produce this ridiculous spurt of guilt?

He could serve his country in other ways, she argued fiercely. A whole alphabet soup of governmental agencies in Washington would snap up someone with his smarts and experience. The Pentagon could put him to work, not to mention the FAA, the CAB and the NTSB.

And not just to fly a desk. Luke could still strap on an airplane if he wanted to. Okay, maybe not a sleek bomber designed to penetrate unseen to the heart of any conflict. But flying was flying.

Yeah, right. Like taking a rowboat out on a small, placid pond was the same as crashing through a rocky gorge on a swollen river.

Well, hell! Why did love have to be so complicated? Lips pursed, Dayna stalked into the bedroom.

Jilly paused in the act of slathering cream on her face and blinked.

"What's wrong?"

"Luke just told me he loves me."

Not in those exact words, but close enough.

Jilly blinked again. "And that pisses you off because…?"

"Because I love him, too, dammit."

The next morning, Luke rapped on the door to Dayna's suite just as she geared up for the final round of the Women's International Pro-Am Charity Tournament.

He'd swung by his flat first to shower and shave. His dark hair still glistened and he'd splashed on a woodsy aftershave that smelled nothing like gardenias. In khaki slacks, a sky-blue V-necked sweater and his leather jacket, he looked good enough to eat.

Dayna almost did just that. She'd had all night to mull over their renegotiations. Glee had vanquished guilt. Her heart flaming with a fiery mix of love and lust, she hooked her arms around his neck and dragged him down for a kiss that left her gasping and him groaning.

"What time do you tee off?"

"Too soon for what either of you have in mind," Jilly drawled from behind them.

"Later," he promised, rubbing Dayna's nose in an Eskimo kiss.

"Later," she breathed, knowing that could mean three long months *if* the Wus went through with their triple deception and *if* Dayna boarded the plane to the States with them and *if* Luke followed through with his plans and *if*...

Oh, hell! She'd had enough *if*s to last a lifetime. What she needed now was action!

"Ready to implement the final phase of Operation Wu?"

Grinning, Luke slung her gear bag over her shoulder. "Let's go get 'em."

When Dayna and her partner, Allison Kendall, joined Joan Ryson-Smith and Kim Li on the first tee, the Korean barely glanced their way.

Nervous and skittish as a racehorse at the starting gate, the teen turned her back on the others and sliced her driver through the air in repeated practice swings. An eager fan edged too close once again and—once again—earned a sharp rebuke. The green-coated official who had the effrontery to suggest she move off the tee box to practice her swing received an icy glare. When her drive went into gorse to the right of the fairway, Kim Li let loose with a spate of angry Korean and stalked off without waiting for the others.

"And this is just the first hole," Allison murmured.

"Should be a fun round," Dayna agreed.

Contrary to expectations, she and Allison soon discovered Kim Li's nervous energy presaged an absolutely brilliant game. After the first bungled drive, the girl hit magnificent shot after shot and sank unbelievable putts. Almost, Dayna thought as they rounded the turn and started the back nine, as though Kim Li had decided to make her final appearance on the circuit as a North Korean golfer one to remember.

The game would certainly stick in Dayna's memory. Every nerve in her body snapping, she managed to hold her own on the links while keeping tabs on the gallery. She connected silently with Luke before every drive. She also recognized several of the undercover British operatives salted through the crowd, or thought she did.

A signal from Hawk confirming the chopper the Wus had requested was in place almost made her whiff her approach shot on number twelve.

Okay. All right. One Wu about to be accounted for. Maybe. Now, for the other two.

Watching from the corner of her eye, Dayna saw Hawk and Jilly edge closer to Dr. Wu.

They moved in on seventeen, then got lost with the doc amid the whooping, surging crowd when Kim Li sank a birdie putt on eighteen to win the round.

Dayna's pulse kicked up several notches. Hawk and Jilly were on the move with their target. Time to do the same with hers.

Except Kim Li looked as though she was having a serious bout of cold feet. The girl stood stone-still on the eighteenth green, accepting the cheers of the crowd with none of her usual verve. Her expression wavered between bravado and apprehension. Dayna could almost smell fear emanating from her.

Disguising her own mounting tension, she hurried across the green and extended her hand. "Congratulations, Kim Li. Fantastic game."

Damp sweat filmed the Korean's palm. Her face had lost every trace of color. "I—I—"

Whatever she was trying to say was lost when a TV crew stuck a camera in her face. A shudder rippled through her, but she pulled herself together and flashed one of her trademark victory grins.

The interview took only a few moments.

Dayna's mind churned the whole while. Had the girl lost her nerve? Or had she and her father staged this whole scene, from start to finish? If so, what was the deal with the chopper? And where were Hawk and Jilly and Dr. Wu?

The sudden, silent vibration against her wrist answered that. The pulsing lasted for ten seconds. Stopped. Began again. Stopped.

Yes! They were in the car and on their way.

Trailed at a discreet distance, she guessed grimly, by Wu's watchdogs. They, too, had disappeared. They wouldn't interfere, though, as long as the scientist played his assigned role of supposed defector.

Craning her neck, Dayna spotted Luke making his way toward her. He stood at her side while Kim Li accepted the trophy and, in turn, presented a check for the funds raised during the tournament to a representative of the International Red Cross. The presentation complete, the girl searched the crowd.

The crunch point was at hand. Was she, too, playing a role? Did she intend to accompany Dayna or retreat to her own country?

As it had on the eighteenth green, her glance locked with Dayna's. The message was unequivocal, if scared as hell.

Dayna keyed her watch to relay a voice signal.

"It's showtime."

That was the cue for highly skilled MI-6 operatives to move into place. Two amiable Scots in tartan vests blocked the path of Kim Li's burly trainer. A tall, svelte blonde waylaid her manager, begging for an interview with the golf star.

Luke, Dayna and Kim Li bypassed the hordes of reporters waiting in the media center and ducked into a nondescript vehicle driven by a cheerful Brit.

"Off we go, then."

With another vehicle in the lead and one behind, they maneuvered St. Andrews' narrow streets. Disaster struck mere moments after Dayna had congratulated herself on a neat extraction.

Chapter 16

The first indication of trouble was the traffic jam the motorcade hit mere blocks from the golf course. The second was the sudden crackle from their vehicle's radio. A disembodied female voice identified herself as field control and requested the driver pick up immediately.

"Duggan here. What's up, luv?"

"We've got reports of a crowd forming quayside. A gathering of antiwar protestors, complete with ban-the-bomb signs and banners."

"The *Dumfries Gazette* group?"

"That's our initial reading."

"Ach, they're harmless."

"Harmless, but noisy. They're attracting quite a crowd."

They were also holding up traffic. Seated beside Kim Li in the backseat, Dayna gave no indication that her nerves were crawling. When their lead vehicle slowed to a near stop, however, she had to notify Hawk. Kim Li watched, white-faced and scared, while Dayna signaled her partner.

"This is Rogue. We've hit traffic. There's a demonstration down by the river."

"We saw the crowd forming when we crossed the bridge."

"Where are you now?"

"Just approaching RAF Leuchars. Keep me posted on your progress."

"Roger."

Kim Li's frightened eyes and trembling hands begged for reassurance.

"We'll get you to the base," Dayna told her calmly.

One way or another.

The traffic tangle grew to a snarl. Their vehicle inched forward for another few minutes, then came to a dead stop along with those ahead and behind. Windows opened for impatient drivers to stick their heads out and crane to see the obstacle. Horns honked. The blare of a loudspeaker sounded above the din, amplifying a strident female voice.

"Do ye want this plasma separator in yer backyard?"

"Sounds like our friend, Ms. Brodie," Luke said. "Alan Parks did his work well last night."

Too well, Dayna thought as Eileen Brodie worked the crowd.

"Do ye care if yer government has lied to ye? Again!"

A rumble of *No*s filled the air.

"We'll tramp the hills until we find this storage facility," she shouted into the mike. "Are ye with us?"

*Aye*s boomed across the car roofs.

"She's gaining steam," the driver commented.

"And we're going nowhere," Dayna muttered, twisting around to check the rear window.

"Rogue, this is Lightning. Come in, please."

She fumbled for her watch. "Go ahead."

"Pick up complete. Madam Wu is aboard the chopper and has just spoken to her husband."

Beside her, Kim Li gave a shriek of joy.

"I have Ms. Wu on the net. She wants to talk to her daughter."

"She's right here."

Static filled the air. While Luke and the driver divided their attention between the bridge just ahead and the logjam behind, Dayna extended her wrist.

"Mama?"

More static. Kim Li's voice spiraled into a desperate cry.

"Mama?"

A spate of Korean shattered the gut-wrenching tension. Laughing, crying, almost incoherent with joy, Kim Li replied in kind.

Before she'd finished, one of the MI-6 operatives in the chase car jumped out and sprinted forward. Wrenching open the passenger door, he gave them unwelcome news.

"We're picking up chatter on the radio."

Code for the bad guys knew something was up and were closing in. Dayna didn't have to interpret for Kim Li or Luke. The operative's tone said it all.

"We've called for another car," he informed them. "It's waiting on the west side of the river. I suggest we cross the bridge on foot."

Luke was out of the car before the British operative finished. Kim Li scrambled out with Dayna.

They almost made it.

With the Brits as escort, Dayna, Luke and Kim Li plunged past the stalled vehicles and down the steep street leading to the bridge. Once there, they discovered access to it was completely blocked. Ms. Brodie and her band had begun their march. Signs bobbing, banners fluttering, they tramped by en masse.

"We'll have to go through them," Dayna said, searching for a break in the phalanx.

It came a moment later. She grabbed one of Kim Li's arms, Luke the other. Together, they shoved a path through the protestors and burst onto the old stone bridge.

The marchers had backed bridge traffic up, as well. Engines idled and growled. Exhaust fumes stunk up the air. Halfway across, Luke jerked to a halt.

"Uh-oh. Looks like trouble."

The Brits weren't the only ones with a vehicle on the west side of the river. The team trailing Dr. Wu to the base must have gotten word something was up.

That became obvious when they spotted Kim Li. Pouring out of their car, the four Koreans shouted at her in their language as they raced for the bridge.

Dayna could never say afterward who fired the shot. All she knew was that it created instant chaos. Women screamed, men shouted and a wild stampede ensued.

"What we do?" Kim Li's voice was shrill with terror.

They had mere seconds to decide. The Koreans were forcing their way through the stalled vehicles dead ahead. The stampeding crowd battered at them from behind.

Dayna had her weapon out but hesitated to fire for

fear of hitting someone in the panicked mob. Luke and the two Brits faced a similar dilemma.

"What do we do?" Kim Li cried again, panic infusing every syllable.

Dayna glanced over the bridge wall at the dark water below.

"We swim," she told Kim Li.

"Swim? No! No! I cannot!"

Dayna's eyes locked with Luke's.

"We can," he said.

Ignoring the girl's frantic protests, they hauled Kim Li toward the low wall edging the bridge.

Dayna stripped off her jacket. The river below was dark and running fast with the tide, but clear of boat traffic. Kicking out of her shoes, she prepared to launch.

"You haven't forgotten how to swim parallel to a swift current?" she threw at Luke.

"How could I?" He reinforced the retort with a grin. "I was taught by an Olympic gold medalist. Up you go."

That last was directed at Kim Li. She bucked out of his hold. "No! I do not… I cannot…"

Scooping her up, Luke tossed her over the low wall. "Nooo!"

Her scream ended when she splashed into the water and went under. Dayna sliced in not three feet away.

Chapter 17

The River Eden's rushing tidal current carried them to the wide, swirling estuary of St. Andrews Bay.

A British Coast Guard cutter plucked them from the bay almost within sight of the Royal and Ancient Golf Clubhouse. The patrol boat then swept around the headland and deposited the three blanket-wrapped swimmers on shoreline contained within the boundaries of RAF Leuchars.

The cutter's captain had radioed ahead. When his passengers scrambled ashore, they were bundled into a waiting vehicle. The car whisked them directly to the USAF C-21 parked on the taxiway.

Luke shed his blanket and saluted the British air commodore standing at the aircraft with Colonel Anderson, Hawk and a visibly shaken Dr. Wu. Sobbing, Kim Li fell into her father's arms.

Jilly edged around them to greet her friend. "Nice look, Duncan. I especially like the orange kelp draped over your left ear."

Swatting away the seaweed, Dayna lowered her voice to an urgent whisper. "How did it go with Dr. Wu?"

"He more than lived up to his end of the deal. Even before he learned he wife was safe, he used hand gestures to let Hawk and me know there was a camera buried in one earpiece of his glasses and a mike in the other. We made sure Colonel Anderson got the message. And *he* made sure Dr. Wu got a clear shot of the modified B-2 before I tripped over my own feet. The last bit the Koreans heard or saw before the doc's glasses shattered on the asphalt was silly, clumsy me squealing an apology."

"You, my friend, are most definitely OMEGA material."

"So I keep telling Hawk."

Her glance shifted to the operative hustling the Wus onto the sleek executive transport.

"Maybe he'll get the message after we turn the

Wus over to their new handlers and I ask Uncle Nick to break the news that I'm joining your ranks."

"Does your uncle Nick know about that?"

"Not yet."

"Your mom and dad?"

"Nope." Laughter sparkled in her blue eyes. "Want to come home with me and provide backup when I tell them I'm following in their footsteps?"

"No way!"

Maggie Sinclair, code name Chameleon, would take her eldest daughter's foray into the world of spooks and spies in stride, as she took everything else. Adam Ridgeway, Dayna suspected, would rattle Washington, D.C.'s marble monuments.

"You'll have to tell them all by your lonesome. You'll also have to help Hawk with the Wus. I'm not flying back to the States with you."

"When did you decide that?"

"This morning, right after a certain sky jockey informed me he…"

The whine of the jet's engines drowned out the rest of her sentence but Jilly got the gist. So did Hawk when Dayna told him about her change of plans.

"You sure about this?" he boomed over the engine's piercing shrill.

"Absolutely."

Luke joined them then, shouting to be heard over

the decibels that magnified with every revolution. "What's going on?"

"Not me," Dayna yelled.

With a last wave for Hawk and Jilly, she dragged him to the edge of the tarmac.

"You didn't give me a chance to counter your offer when you reopened negotiations this morning."

"Counter?" His hazel eyes darkened. "Don't even think it, lady. You sealed the deal."

"Wait. Hear me out."

Easier to say than do with the jet revved to full power and its exhaust whipping her wet hair into a whirlwind.

"The B-2s are home-based at Whiteman AFB, Missouri, right?"

"When they're not forward deployed."

The jet began to taxi, thank God. Dayna didn't have to bellow to be heard.

"You've only got a few months left on this assignment. Then you'll rotate back to Whiteman. There's a new swift-water training center on the Moose River. I can teach there, as well as in Virginia and work my ops for OMEGA in between."

"I don't know they'll send me to Whiteman. It could be the Pentagon. Or Armed Forces Staff College. Or Pilot Instructor School."

"Wherever it is, we'll make it work."

Luke wanted to crush her against him and shout

hell, yes, they'd make it work, but the past held him in too tight a fist. He'd chosen his military career over Dayna their first time around. Even if he'd made that choice with her dreams as much or more in mind than his own, he knew now the decision had been dead wrong.

That Dayna was willing to work around his military commitments despite the past hurts filled him with a love so fierce he ached with it. Still, he gave her one last out.

"You sure you can live with a man in uniform for the next ten or twenty or fifty years?"

Laughing, she hooked her arms around his neck. "I'll grin and bear it, flyboy. As long as I get you *out* of uniform on a regular basis."

* * * * *

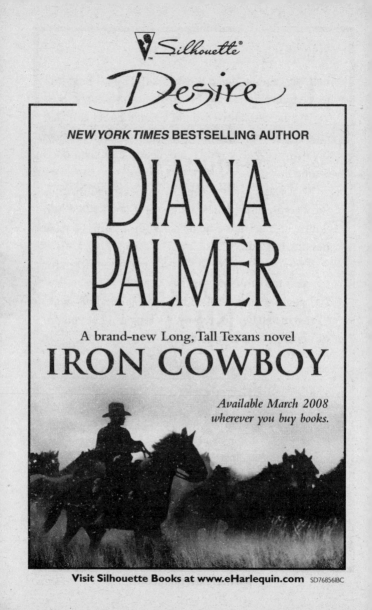

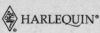

Silhouette®
Romantic
SUSPENSE

COMING NEXT MONTH

#1503 A DOCTOR'S SECRET—Marie Ferrarella
The Doctors Pulaski
Dr. Tania Pulaski vows never to get involved with a patient. Then Jesse
Steele enters her ER. Although he's strong and attractive, she hesitates
taking things to the next level…until someone starts stalking her and
she must trust the one man who can help her.

#1504 THE REBEL PRINCE—Nina Bruhns
Serenity Woodson knows the charismatic and sexy man who's been
helping her aunt must be a con man. Then she learns the incredible
truth—Carch Sunstryker is a prince from another planet, on a mission
to Earth that may save his kingdom. Loving him would be insanity—
but neither can resist the intense attraction that could destroy them
both.

#1505 THE HEART OF A RENEGADE—Loreth Anne White
Shadow Soldiers
After Luke Stone fails to protect his wife and unborn child, he refuses
to take on another bodyguard assignment. But when he becomes the
only man who can protect foreign correspondent Jessica Chan from
death, he faces the biggest challenge of his life…because being so close
to Jessica threatens to break his defenses.

#1506 OPERATION: RESCUE—Anne Woodard
Derrick Marx will do anything to rescue his brother from the terrorists
holding him captive, including kidnapping the reclusive botanist whose
knowledge of the jungle is the key to his success. Against her will,
Elizabeth Bradshaw leads Derrick through the jungle, but quickly finds
the forced intimacy is more dangerous
than the terrorists themselves.

SRSCNM0208